REHAB

Also by Randi Reisfeld

CC (Cape Cod)

Summer Share: Partiers Preferred

• • •

REHAB

RANDI REISFELD

Simon Pulse New York London Toronto Sydney

SIMON PULSE

An imprint of Simon & Schuster Children's Publishing Division

1230 Avenue of the Americas, New York, NY 10020

Copyright © 2008 by Randi Reisfeld

All rights reserved, including the right of reproduction

in whole or in part in any form.

SIMON PULSE and colophon are registered

trademarks of Simon & Schuster, Inc.

Designed by Tom Daly

The text of this book was set in Arrus BT.

Manufactured in the United States of America

First Simon Pulse edition July 2008

10 9 8 7 6 5 4 3 2 1

Library of Congress Control Number 2008922276

ISBN-13: 978-1-4169-6121-5

ISBN-10: 1-4169-6121-6

For Sandy, who always had a twinkle in her eye, a wry smile on her lips, an indomitable spirit, and a heart filled with generosity and love. I miss you, my friend.

REHAB

CHAPTER ONE

". . . And Introducing Kenzie Cross as Morgan Spacey"

"And . . . *action*! We're rolling, people!"

On the director's command, the chalk clapboard clicked and Kenzie Cross slipped into her TV character, undercover spy Morgan Spacey.

"Thanks for getting here so quickly, Jack," Kenzie purred, patting the cushion of the luxe Armani Casa sofa.

"You said it was urgent. What's the emergency?" Jason Victor, the actor playing Jack, delivered his lines coolly, while his eyes roamed over Kenzie's curvy body, encased in a short, ultratight dress.

"There's something we need to do, *in private*." Kenzie was supposed to deliver that line suggestively, cross her legs seductively, signal her intentions, just as she had during the first two takes of that scene.

This time, Kenzie couldn't do it.

The scene made her skin crawl. It was so sleazy, and not at all in keeping with her clever, canny character, Morgan.

Without warning, Kenzie veered off-script.

"We need to talk, Jack," she said instead, drawing herself up, facing him straight on. "Some new information has come to light."

"This is really surprising," the actor responded, trying to hide his confusion. "This is the first time we've been alone in your apartment. You said you weren't ready for . . ." He trailed off with a wink and a sly smile. Practically foaming at the mouth.

"Cut!" The director's voice boomed. Noel Riggs, whose instincts Kenzie usually respected, was obviously unhappy with her ad lib.

"Sorry," Kenzie said, ready to redo the scene as written.

"No need to apologize, Kenzie! You're genius—it's better your way."

Kenzie started to relax, when he dropped the B-bomb: "But . . ."

"What?" she asked warily.

"You're sweating, nervous, uncomfortable. I'm not diggin' it."

Her character, Morgan, *should* be uncomfortable, Kenzie believed. In this episode the supposedly savvy spy had fallen for this Jack character, only to uncover evidence proving him to be a fraud—and a killer. She was setting up a seduction scene as a trap. She *should* be nervous.

Not that Kenzie would ever say that to the director. Rule number one for a newcomer in her first role: Never, ever, disagree with the director.

Have your agent do it for you later.

Kenzie Cross had turned out to be a quick study in all things showbiz. She'd arrived in Hollywood only a year ago and *Spywitness Girls* was her first professional credit; Morgan Spacey, her first role. Ever!

Against all odds, both the show and Kenzie herself had

become breakout hits. Back in September, when it debuted, *Spywitness Girls* got slammed with harsh, negative reviews. Critics dismissed it as nothing more than retread of the old *Charlie's Angels* series. Ratings were poor; pundits placed it on the "about-to-be-canceled" list.

A funny thing happened on the way to oblivion, though.

Internet-savvy fans found the show, blogged about it, and started a viral campaign to support it. Fast-forward eight months to May, and twenty-two episodes later. *Spywitness Girls* lifted, phoenix-like, from the buzz-challenged basement to become bigger than those (super) *Heroes*, found by viewers more times than *Lost,* was chatted about more than *Gossip Girl.*

Of the three glamorous stars, one got singled out as the fan favorite.

Kenzie Cross.

Least experienced, last one cast, petite as an Olsen twin with Fergie-licious curves, the nineteen-year-old newcomer was the people's choice, the hottest starlet guys would most like to date, and girls would most like to hang out with.

Kenzie was surprised only in that it'd happened so quickly. She'd always been popular, a true charisma girl, but that was back home in her Seattle suburb. She thought it'd take way longer to shine in the diamond-dappled pool of Hollywood talent. She was, to say the least, unprepared for what followed.

Fan frenzy led to media madness. Magazines, online columns, and TV entertainment shows wanted her; designers fell all over themselves for the honor of dressing her. All the hot clubs cleared the best tables; offers of big money came at her so quickly, Kenzie felt like the head-spinning girl in *The Exorcist.* Except without the spewing.

She'd also snared the hottest boyfriend in town, underwear model Cole Rafferty. (Swoon, swoon.) They'd met at a club a couple of weeks ago. Their connection was instant, deep in a totally superficial way . . . but still.

Speaking of, thinking of, led her thoughts back to last night. Cole had been a wild man at the new hot spot—Leopoles—dancing, drinking, vibing with her and her friends. And so caring and attentive when she accidentally fell off the stripper pole. It wasn't her fault—it was the damn shoes. The Pradas with those to-die-for heels nearly became the death of her, or at least of her ankle. Which twisted and turned in ways that most joints, especially those needed to hold you upright, should not.

Cole had slipped her a couple painkillers, which she'd downed on the spot. As insurance, she'd popped a few more for breakfast this morning. But by now—Kenzie had been working under the hot lights for hours—they'd worn off. Another reason, though Kenzie would never tell her director, she looked uncomfortable doing the scene.

Director Noel was now signaling they were ready to go. The actors began again, only to get through their first lines before hearing him shout, "Cut!"

Through the camera lens, Noel had noticed beads of sweat across Kenzie's forehead. The director was not "diggin' it." He snapped his fingers, and summoned what Kenzie liked to call the "Beauty Squad." A phalanx of assistants, bearing soft towels, lip gloss and powder, curling iron and electric warming booties, materialized. Bypassing the actor playing

Jack, they were all there to cater to Kenzie. A star's gotta rock the camera, and *that's* a no-sweat zone.

Just then, Chelsea Piers, Kenzie's best friend and personal assistant, rushed onto the set. "Hey, Kenz," she whispered, "does your ankle hurt? Do you need another Vicodin for the pain?"

Oh, man, she was soooo tempted, she could feel herself twitching. Kenzie knew she shouldn't. How many times had she been warned about getting addicted? And yet. She was tired and in pain. She hated the dress, could barely tolerate the actor playing Jack, whose aftershave was to-gag-for *or* from. Whatever, it made her nauseous.

Nailing this particular scene, much as she abhorred it, was crucial. It was the episode ender; the last show of the season, expected to go through the ratings roof. It was huge.

The director had bowed to her way of playing it. She ought to just get it wrapped.

Kenzie quickly swallowed the oblong pill.

Good thing, too, she'd think later. Without the mellow painkiller, she might've spit at "Jack"—on camera. During the break, he'd apparently decided that if Kenzie could ad lib, so could he.

Just as she said the line, "Some new information has come to light," he "spontaneously" pulled her to him, stuck his tongue in her mouth, and cupped her breast—all in one fluid, revolting move.

Not even Cole got away with that unless invited.

And yet, Noel let it go, allowing the scene to play out until the other Spywitness Girls came crashing into the scene, guns blazing, to arrest the unsuspecting pervo-perp.

By that time, the word "Cut!" had never sounded so sweet to Kenzie's ears.

She wiped her mouth off, while the erstwhile "Jack" shot her a self-satisfied, slimy grin. "Surprised ya, huh?"

"Understatement," she groused.

"Aw, come on, Kenzie, look how angry you got. It made the scene work."

Kenzie made herself a promise: If she ever did get more clout on the show, this tool would not be guest-starring on it anytime soon. As in, ever.

Clueless, he gave her that thumb-up, pinky-down signal for "Call me." That's the new "Let's do lunch." It's just as insincere.

The set was packed. Everyone even vaguely connected with *Spywitness Girls* was on hand to bask in the show's success, now that they'd wrapped the final episode for the season. Producers, network suits, studio bigwigs, casting directors, publicists, everyone's agents, managers, spouses, and significant others swarmed the set. It was *Entourage* times a thousand.

Champagne corks popped, and back patting, hugging, shoulder rubs, and air kisses spread like a virus.

Kenzie wished she could slip out the back door, head to her trailer. She was into celebrating as much as the next girl, but not with this bunch of glad-handers. She was looking forward to the weekend, when there'd be a huge wrap party at an exclusive private club. All her friends would be there; she'd be with Cole. *That* would rock!

But pulling a disappearing act now wasn't gonna

happen. There were too many people waiting to see her, specifically the showbiz professionals called Team Kenzie, or her "handlers."

First was tall, tan, regal Alex Grant, super-agent. It was his responsibility to get Kenzie acting roles. The bigger, the better. Alex earned 15 percent of Kenzie's income.

Rudy Marpole, rotund, cherub-cheeked, and often verklempt, was her manager. His job was to oversee her entire career, and guide her appropriately. Rudy's cut of the Kenzie pie was 10 percent.

Rounding out the trio was publicist Milo Prince, a chic she, even though Milo is a trendy name for boys. Her job was to make Kenzie into a household name—in the most positive way a starlet can be known. Milo earned a hefty monthly fee for her services.

Alex was first to congratulate her. "Kenzie! You were amazing. This is why they call you the 'franchise.' Without you, this show doesn't exist."

"A bald-faced lie, but thank you, Alex." Kenzie stood on the tiptoes of her high heels to give her agent a peck on the cheek.

Rudy, a head shorter than Alex, had real tears in his eyes, and was choked with emotion as he wrapped her in a bear hug. "Sweetie pie, you're the icing on the cake with the cherry on top. That's all I can say, Kenzie. You . . . you made that last scene sing."

"Sing? Like an *American Idol* reject maybe," Kenzie quipped. Rudy, unlike Alex, actually believed what he said. Kenzie wasn't sure which she preferred: the slick liar or the earnest doofus. They were both true Hollywood types.

Alex, with a furtive glance around the room, bent to whisper in Kenzie's ear. "I'm hearing good things about your movie audition."

The Chrome Hearts Club. That's what it was called, the ginormous feature film Kenzie had unexpectedly gotten an audition for. Unexpected, because the film was "serious," and she wasn't even on the short list of big-name actresses who might win the starring role. She had Alex to thank for even getting her the audition. But to think she'd win the role was absurd. She was about to give Alex a reality check when a balding, bespectacled TV producer inserted himself between client and agent. A producer whose name Kenzie could not for the life of her recall regaled her with over-the-top compliments.

"I laughed, I cried, OMG, Kenzie, you're the best. So natural!" In his wake, other VIPs followed, variations on the same worshipful theme ensued. Kenzie needed to slip into the role of grateful, modest ingenue.

Kenzie wasn't disingenuous—she truly loved being complimented—but these people acted like she'd won a Nobel Prize based on one lousy scene. It would take a better actress than her to believably bask in the glow of bullshit.

When publicist Milo pulled her away from the adoring masses, Kenzie was sincerely thankful.

"Some others have been waiting to see you," Milo said, pointing toward a gaggle of young fans, herded behind a rope at the back of the soundstage. They were tween girls mostly, armed with cameras, and photos to autograph.

"What did they win?" Kenzie asked as they made their way over.

"An essay contest. It's a 'green' thing. They had to come up with original ideas for saving the planet. The top ten won a meet and greet with you. *People* magazine is covering it."

What tied Kenzie Cross to environmental health was a head-scratcher, but anytime she got to meet the real fans who'd made her a star, she was genuinely psyched.

It wasn't so long ago, she *was* them. Worshipping celebrities, wanting to know all about their glamorous lives, dreaming of one day transforming from a regular, ordinary person to a pedestal-perching, sparkling star. To be the adored, instead of the adoring. That'd been her, circa all her life.

"Hi, everyone—it's so great to meet you!" Kenzie exclaimed, walking from one to the next, shaking hands, getting cheek to cheek with them for their cameras. Kenzie asked questions about recycling, plastic bags, penguins, and hybrids, but basically, all they wanted was to commemorate the moment they'd met a real star. The photographer from *People* snapped away.

When it was over, Kenzie started for her dressing room—then did an impulsive U-turn. Something was bothering her. She couldn't recall what Noel, the director, had said about her performance.

The self-assured starlet kinda wanted his validation.

She found Noel peering into the camera, most likely replaying that last scene. When she tapped him on the shoulder, he whirled around. And smiled.

"You really nailed it for us, Kenzie. We're a lock for next season."

That's it then. All the experts have spoken. If they thought she rocked it—without even liking it, let alone believing it—she must have. She let out the sigh of relief she didn't know she'd been holding in.

CHAPTER TWO

Meet the Peeps

"Hard-partying ingenue Kenzie Cross made the rounds last night—circling from Teddy's to Les Deux to Leopoles on the Strip, downing shots and dancing the night away. Accompanied by her attached-at-the-hip acolytes—scion-turned-club promoter Gabe Waxworth, celebrity hatchling Lev Romano, and, ahem, "personal assistant" Chelsea "Chesty" Piers—Kenzie brought her trademark giggle, sexy wiggle, and (contrary to her wholesome image) overtly sexual moves to all the clubs. She stayed longest and latest at Leopoles, where she stripped down to her skivvies, wrapped herself around the club's signature stripper pole, and belted out Beyoncé's inescapable "Irreplaceable." Word to the wise, Kenzie: No one, including you, is irreplaceable."

Kenzie had just one foot inside her trailer, eager to peel off her restricting dress and take a shower. Her friends Gabe, Lev, and Chelsea were hunched over a laptop. Chelsea was reading aloud from an online column. She looked up when Kenzie came in, explaining. "It's from TMZ."

Of course it is, Kenzie thought. In high school, before

she'd come to Hollywood, TMZ had been the go-to website for the juiciest, most salacious gossip. Back then, they surely weren't writing about her and she loved reading it. Now? Not so much.

She should have expected it, she told herself. Gossip was the downside of fame; stardom was the upside, and stardom was . . . well, inevitable.

Mackenzie Cross, always called Kenzie, not only dreamed about stardom, she grew up with the absolute knowledge of it.

Mostly everyone not directly related to her disagreed. What shot did she have? She lived outside of Seattle; the Cross clan had no connections, and not a lot of disposable income. To be clear: Kenzie was not *My Super Sweet 16* bait; she had little access to plastic, let alone cosmetic improvements. No one was going to wave a magic wand or a black AmEx card and whisk her off to Hollywood.

The girl was small-time.

The big dreams had come courtesy of her mom, but once that situation fizzled, Kenzie had to settle for the local drama coach, dancing class, piano and singing lessons. She performed in school plays and community theater, with her head up, tatas out, optimism undaunted.

Teachers, neighbors, and occasionally the cops had serious reservations about Kenzie ever making it out of Seattle, let alone all the way to Hollywood. They tsk-tsked her partying, the revolving-door boyfriends, staying out late on school nights instead of studying. The nonbelievers pegged her as "most likely to end up reciting today's specials at Hooters."

None of that fazed her. Her dad was a Kenzie-believer;

her younger brother, Seth, worshipped her. Most important, she believed in herself.

Kenzie knew her strengths. She could be a really good actress, given the right part. Plus, she attracted people like ants to a picnic.

Partly it was her looks. Guys found her irresistible, a hottie with a tawny-bronze complexion, long blond hair, huge swimming-pool-blue eyes that were, her dad used to joke, "The size of salad plates."

And partly it was her personality. She was friendly to everyone (even the nerds and losers), she never flaunted her A-list status (was not a bitch), was funny, smart, outgoing, and threw the best parties.

Everyone in high school had wanted in on "orbit Kenzie."

Kenzie wanted in on "orbit showbiz."

When it happened for her, thanks to her inventive series of webisodes on YouTube, one of her Seattle buds actually did come with.

Kenzie Cross and Chelsea Piers grew up on the same block. In grade school they'd become BFFs, always together, so close that Kenzie's dad used to call them "Mac & Cheese," for Mackenzie and Chelsea.

It felt natural that when Kenzie, eighteen at the time, got cast in *Spywitness Girls,* and moved to Los Angeles, Chelsea would come along. Kenzie dubbed her a "personal assistant," and paid her well for the "job" she'd always done: being her best friend. These days, there were amazing perks to Chelsea's job. The buxom brunette shared the freebies that came Kenzie's way: luxe designer duds and eye-popping accessories. Chelsea got in to all the cool parties, hung out in private clubs, and met stars. It was like living inside the pages of *Us Weekly*.

The girls had met club scenesters Lev Romano and Gabe Waxworth at a party their first week in L.A. Over bottle service and banquette dancing, the foursome had connected.

That'd been last summer. Now, just shy of a year later, the guys had become Kenzie and Chelsea's most trusted allies, the inner circle.

Right now, said peeps were relaxing in Kenzie's trailer, taking turns reading aloud from the gossip blogs and the tabloids. The one from TMZ had recapped last night's antics pretty accurately. Good thing they missed the Vicodin washed down with Ketel One, but Chelsea knitted her brows. "What do they mean by her '*ahem*, personal assistant'?"

"They're insinuating that you and Kenzie are friends of Ellen," cracked Lev, whose lean frame filled a tall, plush armchair. "You know, gay."

"You should be flattered. They just put you in the same category as Oprah and Gayle," Gabe pointed out.

Kenzie chuckled. She used to assume it was only fans devouring tabloids and gossip blogs. But supermarket shoppers and web surfers had nothing on actual Hollywood scenesters and celebrities. They read everything that was written about them. It was like their lives weren't real unless they were mentioned in the media.

She decided against overthinking that concept.

"'Kenzie Cross—Partying Too Much? Will everyone's favorite shooting star fade too soon, become a falling

star? My spies caught her at Leopoles on Sunset, the newest hot spot on the Strip, where she switched clothes with the dancers . . . '"

Time to tune out. Kenzie knew how this one from Hollywood.com ended. Besides, the writer had answered her own question. As long as the tabloids kept covering Kenzie's every move, fading away anytime soon wasn't likely. She retreated to her private bedroom and peeled the tiny sticky dress off. Maybe she'd donate it to a needy toddler.

Not so long time ago, she'd worn secondhand clothes.

These days, Kenzie needed for nothing.

Halfway through the *Spywitness Girls* season, when everyone realized how popular Kenzie was becoming, the producers "incentivized" her (a bribe, basically, to ensure her loyalty) by paying her a lot more money, as well as giving her a sleek, silver Airstream trailer to use as a dressing room. It was more like a luxe mobile home: big enough for a full-sized and well-stocked kitchen, a living room, and a private bedroom with its own bathroom.

The giving-of-the-Airstream made Kenzie an envy target.

Her costars, Amber Blue and Romy Dumesque, the other Spywitness Girls, relegated to mere dressing rooms on the set, were incensed. They demanded upgrades—only to be told *they* were replaceable.

Kenzie felt guilty about the whole thing. To her, Amber and Romy were every bit as talented as she was—more sophisticated, genuine beauties, in fact. That viewers had chosen her over them in popularity . . . well, it wasn't her fault.

Still, she badly wanted to say something, make a peace offering. Something like "We'll share the trailer. We can rotate—each use it for a few months." She would have done it, but agent Alex nixed the idea. He'd acted personally offended, sniffing, "Kenzie, if you can't take being treated like a star, get out of the Porsche." (Word had it, Alex was angling to get her a free sports car from the producers.)

After that, Kenzie hadn't known how to act toward Amber and Romy. They had no such problem. They simply iced her.

Maybe next season, she thought, but in no way believed, one of them would be the popularity-magnet, and get her own trailer.

"*Exclusive to the* Enquirer! *Kenzie Caught Canoodling! She fronts she's with underwear model Cole Rafferty, but the proof is in the pictures. Check it out: Last night at Leopoles, our eagle-eyed photographer found a sloshed and slovenly Kenzie Cross getting busy in a back booth, with her newest boy-toy, Lev Romano, a charter member of Slackers Ubiquitous. Imagine how proud his hardworking parents, Los Angeles Opera stars Angelo and Cecilia Romano, must be!*'"

Chelsea was reading aloud when Kenzie returned to the living room, showered, toweled off, refreshed.

She caught Lev's look. He was trying not to show it, but the item rankled him. Gabe, on the other hand, was completely transparent in his glee. He pumped his wiry fist in the air, triumphantly. "This is sick, every single column mentioned Leopoles! It's better than if I wrote them all myself."

"Did you?" Lev asked. "'Cause I wouldn't put it past you, dude."

"Awesome, Gabe!" Kenzie congratulated her friend. "This calls for a toast."

"I'm on it." Lev made a beeline for the fridge.

Kenzie was sincerely proud of Gabe. The boy was only twenty-one and already the hottest club promoter in town. He did come from a superrich family; what'd been reported in TMZ was true, but Gabe was all about making it on his own. Kenzie supported that.

Not just in concept, either. She helped him.

Since most people want to be where stars hang out, whenever she appeared at one of Gabe's clubs, other young stars inevitably followed, and the club became the new hot hangout. Business boomed. Kenzie & company got the best tables, primo bottles of booze, were never carded nor charged. Best of all, Gabe snared a nice commission, and proved to his family he didn't need their money.

Totally win-win. Kenzie was glad to be part of it.

As for the stuff written about her personally? It hadn't taken her long to learn to let it roll. Most of it was exaggerated anyway, though that's not what she'd say if asked in a TV interview. She'd protest it was all a bunch of lies. In other words, *she'd* lie.

That was how the game was played. Tabloid tattlers, pesky paparazzi, it's the price you pay for fabulous fame, fortune, living your dream. Her dad always said nothing in life is free. She thought of it like paying the toll collector so you can get onto the freeway with the fast lane. Or paying two hundred dollars to pass "Go" in Monopoly. It's what's done here.

This particular *Enquirer* exclusive, however, was tougher to brush off. When she and Lev had made out, they'd been . . . not so sober. Cole had wandered away, Lev saw a paparazzo approaching, and screwing with the guy had seemed like what Ashton does on his show, *Pop Culture*. A fun goof, just to prove that papar-idiots would believe anything.

Only now, in the cold hard light of sobriety? Kenzie wondered if Cole realized it was just a joke. Lev, she could tell, was feeling ambushed by the crack about his parents.

Result? The joke had backfired. Time for a beer. Or three.

The friends settled in and toasted Gabe, over and over. Kenzie hoped Cole would show up. He'd said he might, and she kinda needed assurance he knew the make-out session was bogus.

"Kenz, you're not listening," Chelsea gently scolded her.

"Huh?" Kenzie had just drained her second beer, the Vicodin was in full effect, and she was settling into a lovely, lazy buzz.

"You got a bunch of messages when you were on-set. Don't you want to hear them?"

"Sorry, Chels. Just tell me the important ones, okay?"

"Your dad called twice, and Seth, once," she recited. "Both to remind you about Seth's soccer game. You said you'd go."

Obviousity. Of course she'd go. Soccer was the biggest thing in her ten-year-old brother's life. He puffed up like that cartoon Michelin man when his star-sister attended his games. "Can you make sure it's on my calendar?" she asked Chelsea.

"You're already booked on a flight up there."

"You rule, Chels. Anything else I should know about?"

"Saved the best for last," she said with a mischievous smile.

"Cole called?" Kenzie guessed.

"Better. The Ferragamo people called. A certain pebbled-calfskin shoulder bag you ordered is coming by messenger today. You are getting it first."

"Stop! No way! The list for that bag is crazy long. Everyone in Hollywood wants it." Kenzie's newfound stardom was one thing, but she'd read in *In Touch* and *InStyle* that A-listers like Charlize and Scarlett coveted that bag. Why was she getting it first?

"Everyone in Hollywood is not the 'it' girl. To the 'it' girl goes the 'it' bag," Lev, slightly tipsy, pronounced.

"She's not the 'it' girl," Gabe corrected Lev, "she's the 'next big thing.' That's better."

Kenzie felt weird being called that, like people expected perfection whether she was out for a Starbucks run or a red-carpet appearance. She had to be careful not to make a misstep, anything that might taint her bright, shiny new image. That paled, though, in comparison to being treated like royalty, like in the ridiculously expensive bag-snaring game, she outranked so many celebrated stars. Would she ever get used to it?

"You can borrow the 'it' bag whenever you want," she quickly told Chelsea. Sharing her stardom-gotten booty with her friends was a major plus. Speaking of sharing, and friends, and uh . . . booty . . . Kenzie fell into her obsession-du-boy: "Did Cole call?"

Chelsea frowned. Translation: yes. Chelsea was not a Cole fan. She insisted he was a serial suck-up—into Kenzie *only* because of her current status. Kenzie didn't believe it. She could tell when a guy was really into her: Cole was. He didn't fawn or bring flowers or text mushy stuff, but he liked the same things she did, dancing, chilling, going out, having fun.

They blended, photogenically speaking, Cole being the ripped, tan muscle-boy model with the shoulder-length, streaked blond hair; Kenzie the curvy, blond TV star with the ever-ready smile and twinkling eyes. They looked good on each other. It wouldn't be long before they'd get a nickname like Zanessa or Brangelina. Kenzie wanted Kenco. Better than Coken.

Things were going well in the career-matchup department. She was the star of a hit TV series; he had a new billboard for boy-thongs on which his body looked like carved marble.

None of which impressed Chelsea. "He wears guy-liner! He puts lifts in his shoes and I just bet he stuffs his—"

That last bit, Kenzie could've told her, was not true.

"Stop stalling, Chels, what did Cole say?"

"That he got held up, he can't see you this afternoon, he'll catch you later at Les Deux. Or, as he pronounces it, Lay Doo. Which probably refers to his two favorite things to do there."

"So he didn't take high school French." Kenzie waved her off. "Trust me. There are other areas in which he excels."

"Sorry, Kenz. But it's in the best friend rule book that I make sure you don't get hurt. Being the 'next big thing,' can't protect you from everything, you know."

"You can act just like a fool, people think
you're cool, just 'cause you're on TV . . ."

—Brad Paisley, "Celebrity"

"Hey! Hey! You! You! I don't like your girlfriend!" Kenzie and Chelsea sang at the top of their lungs, dancing sexily, pointing their fingers at hot guys every time Avril belted out, "You! You!"

It was an admittedly cheesy dance move that Kenzie and Chelsea had started back in high school, dance-flirting with jocks and homecoming kings. They were doing the same thing now, only the "flirtees" were famous—club kids, actors, rockers, hip-hoppers, and models. The girlfriends had traded up.

The weekend had finally arrived and with it, the *Spywitness Girls* wrap party. The wrap party was a Hollywood tradition invented to celebrate the end of a film or TV season. Mostly, it was an excuse to party until dawn, schmooze, see and be seen, hook up, and get crazy, all on someone else's tab. The *Spywitness Girls* fiesta was being held at Radar, Gabe's newest club client. Tonight was a full-out blast. DJ Skratch, the most in-demand spinner in town, had brought his A-game; name-brand drinks were flowing, and the guest list was total glitterati. Those who weren't dancing, drinking, or showing off were getting cozy in dimly lit corners or getting high in the VIP room.

It was a private party, jam-packed to the rafters. Everyone who had anything to do with the show was there, cast, crew, producers, studio reps, all the guest stars on during the season—plus everyone's assistants, friends, family. Famous faces were everywhere, aided and abetted by a swell of Hollywood scensters, toned, tanned, and tipsy.

So her scene, Kenzie thought as she arrived late, exactly on schedule. She fit in and stood out at the same time, as befitting the star of the show. She wore one of the outfits she'd been allowed to keep from her very first *ELLEgirl* photo shoot—a thigh-grazing, sparkly baby-doll dress. Her stylist had found an amazing pair of shiny ruby-colored Viktor & Rolf high heels to go with. (Even though Britney, circa the lunatic years, nearly ruined it for everyone, most fashion magazine editors let celebrities keep anything they like. Kenzie remembered once hearing that if you do a lot of magazine photo shoots, you can end up with racks and racks of amazing ensembles, enough to fill ten closets.)

"Hey, girlfriend, having fun yet?" Chelsea hip checked Kenzie when the song ended. Chels, swilling champagne and rocking a sequined mini, was both sparkly *and* sweaty.

"I'd be having a better time if Cole were here," Kenzie admitted.

"Your knight in shining Armani?" she cracked. "He is here. At the bar, chatting up some random Vanessa, or Ninessa or Vynessa. Whoever got the most press today."

Kenzie took off in the direction of the bar, but never got there—she kept bumping into people she knew and stopping to talk. Then "Party Like a Rock Star" came on and Chelsea materialized, dragging her onto the dance floor. Kenzie easily slid into dance-and-flirt mode. She was doing just that with a cute actor who'd guest-starred on the show when she felt strong, familiar fingers grip her waist. She turned around slowly.

"Cole. So the rumor is true. You are here." She aimed to sound casual, but not even. He was drop-dead gorgeous, his Armani shirt unbuttoned to display his chiseled pecs. His freshly washed surfer hair was fetchingly tucked behind his ears. Only his eyes, usually steely and bright, betrayed time spent at the bar.

"I just got here and was watching you dance," he said now.

Sure you were, Kenzie thought. She believed Chelsea over him, but now that he was here . . . she couldn't help it, she let it go. Instead of challenging him, she asked coyly, "Did you like what you saw?"

"Let's go up to the VIP room, and I'll show you how much." His eyes roamed her body hungrily. Something about the way he acted reminded her of that last scene she'd filmed—the Jack character had that same skeevy look in his eyes. Unintentionally, Cole made it worse by pulling her close to him and cupping her breast.

The flashback was an instant buzzkill.

"Let's get a drink," Kenzie suggested, leading him over to her table, where Lev and a friend were downing shots of tequila. Lev was lit like a blinged-out rapper, but he looked so cute with his hair in his eyes, Kenzie grinned.

"Cheers!" Lev raised his shot glass, but the liquor missed his mouth, and everyone cracked up.

"What number is that?" Kenzie asked suspiciously.

"Let's just say, Kenz, you and your real boy-toy have some catching up to do."

At the mention of "real" boy-toy, Cole smooched her. Never for a moment had he believed the tabloid-show-and-tale about Kenzie and Lev. Or, as Chelsea saw it: "His name was mentioned, and that's all he cared about."

Lev hiccupped, then snapped his fingers. A waiter materialized carrying a tray with two bottles of Patron.

"Wow," she said, impressed, "They read minds here. Very cool."

"But if they could only read yours, Kenzie-penzie-pie," Lev slurred. When he went to pour, his hand was shaking.

"Lev, babe, you better pace yourself," Kenzie warned, wondering if she should be alarmed. "This night is just getting started."

"Not a prob," he assured her, "especially if you two hurry and catch up."

Kenzie didn't think she wanted to catch up with Lev—that boy was hammered. She drank only socially (albeit, these days, that meant nightly), not nearly as much as the tabloids made out. The thing was: Kenzie was small, just over five feet tall, and it didn't take very many drinks to get her drunk.

She and Cole did a few shots, and after the usual throat-on-fire feeling, she felt nice and loosey-goosey, and almost changed her mind about Cole and the privacy of the VIP room.

"Can I get a shot of the three of you?" They hadn't seen the photographer appear.

Kenzie grimaced. She'd forgotten that select photogs

were allowed at the party for a limited time. Cooperation was a given.

Obligingly, the threesome put their heads together and smiled. The photographer sneered, "So Kenzie, which one is your boyfriend? The slacker or the himbo? Or are you doing both?"

Her jaw dropped. What an asshole!

"Wouldn't you like to know." Cole played along idiotically. He grabbed Kenzie and kissed her really hard. Openmouthed and slobbering with saliva. If that wasn't revolting enough, he reached behind her, grabbed Lev's hand and pressed it onto Kenzie's butt.

Lev, though polluted, saved the day. Her *Spywitness Girls* costars, Amber and Romy, must have smelled camera: They were almost upon the group when Lev motioned them over. He teased the skeev-o-razzo, "If you're digging for dirt, here's the real scoop. Secretly, we're all doing each other!"

Amber and Romy, in spray-on tans and minidresses, stuck their best assets out, but that photo would never run. Eventually, even the dumbest photographers know when they're being played.

When the lensman left, Kenzie confronted Cole. "What was that about?"

"You and Lev mess with the paparazzi, what's the problem?"

"Cole, what you just did? Not cool."

Cole held his palms up. "Whoa, sorry, Kenzie. I didn't mean to upset you. That's the last thing I'd want to do." He embraced her, hugged her to his exposed chest, and kissed the top of her head. "Let me make it up to you. The right way." He nodded toward the VIP room.

This wasn't the first time he'd apologized to her. Cole gives good "my bad," always sounding sincere, sweet. Kenzie hadn't been able to stay mad, not even once. Tonight, with all she'd had to drink, she was finding it hard to even remember why she was supposed to be mad in the first place.

She began to kiss Cole, when who should butt in—accent on the "butt"—but Amber. "What's this I'm hearin' about you being a movie star now?"

It was more accusation than question. It threw Kenzie.

"Word is, you're starring in a big movie during hiatus. Thought maybe you'd have the courtesy to tell me and Romy yourself, instead of us having to hear it like some rumor."

Kenzie calculated: Amber + booze = jealous *and* belligerent.

Kenzie refused to defend herself. She held her ground, acknowledged her audition for *The Chrome Hearts Club.*

Amber narrowed her hazel eyes. "What's it about?"

Although Kenzie hadn't read the entire script, her agent and her manager had filled her in on the basics. "A group of outsider kids, juvies," was all she decided to tell Amber.

"And *you* landed the lead role?" Amber questioned, not kindly.

Kenzie cast a sideways glance at Cole. It'd be sweet if he'd say something, better if he just swept her away from this awkward situation. Lev would have. But Cole's canny eyes were elsewhere, sweeping the girls on the dance floor. Kenzie's annoyance fueled her retort.

"Listen, Amber, I only auditioned for it, and *I* heard," Kenzie flat-out lied, "that Chloe Sevigny, Natalie Portman, and Ellen Page—that girl from *Juno*—are also up for it, so take your jealously and stick it between your—"

Amber's lip-lined mouth opened. Kenzie suddenly wanted to take back her nasty words, but Amber didn't give her the chance. She stomped off.

Next season on Spywitness Girls! Kenzie did a mental promo: *Amber murders Kenzie!*

Someone grabbed her hand. Not Cole.

"This is our favorite song!" Chelsea shouted. "You have to dance, Kenzie!"

She was right. On both counts. They sang it loud, danced it proud: *"They tried to make me go to rehab but I said, no, no, no."*

The place was raging. Waiters with bottles of champagne, vodka, and tequila roamed the room. Lev grabbed a bottle of vodka, took a swig, wiped his mouth on his arm, and passed it on.

"I won't go! Go! Go!" Kenzie yelled, chugging the steely-tasting stuff. "Oh my God, how much fun-rony is this? Hey, guys, listen, I made up a new word!" She shouted over the music as the bottle made its way from her to Chelsea, then Gabe, and back to Lev.

"Fun-rony: fun and irony combined," Kenzie bellowed, "'cause we're getting toasted and singing about rehab! Am'int I clever?"

"Am'int you hammered," Chelsea pointed out, giggling. "Who needs college—we speak English all good!"

It was—they were—all good. Even though, as the party

picked up steam, she lost sight of Cole; even though Amber had been harsh, and she harsher, Kenzie landed on her dancing feet, surrounded by her closest friends.

"Look at her," Chelsea whispered when the group took a dance break, pointing at Kenzie's other costar, Romy. "If her breasts were pushed up any higher, she could rest her chin on them."

"Or we could use them as a tray," Lev laughed drunkenly. "Let's go see if we can balance a shot glass on them."

Kenzie pulled him back.

Injuring one costar a night was her limit. Anyway, Lev would have regretted this in the morning, and friends don't let friends . . . regret stuff. Or something. It's what she'd been telling her dad, whenever he freaked out about the tabloid stuff: She had friends to keep her stable, sane, steady. Like just before, Lev totally saved Kenzie from an embarrassing situation; she saved him from one now. She helps Gabe; Gabe helps her. As for Chelsea, always the best.

"You guys are so sweet," she blurted. "Without you, I wouldn't be here." She hiccupped. Belched maybe. Must have been closer to DJ Skratch's mike than she realized, 'cause the belch echoed around the club, reducing everyone to belly laughs.

They were having so much fun, were so trashed, Kenzie thought she was hallucinating, because three people who shouldn't have been in the house, were. Alex, Rudy, and Milo beamed in like a holograph right in front of Kenzie's table. Their mouths were moving, but she couldn't hear above the music, nor think clearly through the haze surrounding her brain.

Chelsea was faster on the uptake, rising to hug Team Kenzie, offering them a round of drinks.

So if she wasn't hallucinating, what exactly were her team of advisors doing there, in the flesh, at two thirty in the morning?

The usually slick, somber Alex was grinning wildly, but it was a red-faced Rudy who burst out with it. "You got the movie!"

"I did?" Kenzie asked, wondering if everyone heard her brain fart. 'Cause for a split second, they'd lost her.

"The studio held an unprecedented all-night casting meeting for *The Chrome Hearts Club.* Filming starts next week. We got you the lead!" Alex crowed.

Kenzie couldn't speak, but Chelsea was on it. She squeezed Kenzie's shoulders. "Focus, K, this is major. The movie!"

Kenzie felt like her brain cells were a kalideoscope: She needed to arrange the pieces so she could see straight. To process. She should probably scream, "Yessss!", jump in the air, hug Alex, Rudy, Milo. Instead, she froze, ambushed by a wave of terror so massive, she nearly keeled over (which could have been the booze, too). She gripped Rudy's arm for support, looked up into his watery blue eyes, heard her own voice quaver. "But I . . . I . . . I'm not worthy! I mean, am I worthy?"

In vino veritas, and truth serum, all in one: She'd hit the lottery getting *Spywitness Girls*, was already living her dream. It was kind of enough, wasn't it? Kenzie wasn't sure she wanted more.

Rudy wrapped a chubby, reassuring arm around her. "Don't go all self-doubting now. The director, Daniel Lightstorm, fought for you. He wants you."

Chelsea must have summoned Lev and Gabe, because all at once, they were hugging her, smothering her with congratulatory kisses.

Her moment of soul-searing doubt evaporated, but Kenzie remained woozy, skeptical. She looked up at tall, slick Alex. "I'm not being punked, am I?"

"Oh, please, Kenzie. 'Punked' is so 2005! This is now."

This is real. "They really think I can do it?" she whispered. "Oh. My. God. I don't believe this is happening to me." Then, she whooped, "Ahhhhh!!"

"I got you the audition," Alex congratulated himself, "but you did the rest."

She was reeling, wanting to cry, "Help! I need help!" Her heart was in overdrive, her head, still in the Land of the Boozed 'n' Confused: "I need to calm down! No, I need to dance! I need—"

She stopped. Where was Cole? Unsteadily, Kenzie hoisted herself up on the nearest banquette to scout him out. He was at the bar. His arms were around some random model. His open mouth was on hers.

Kenzie swallowed and slunk down. The pin was *thisclose* to her balloon—but no. It was her party; it was her moment. She'd be damned if she'd cry.

"Forget about him." Chelsea clamped her hands on Kenzie's shoulders, forcing her to turn away.

Later, Kenzie would remember with gratitude that Chelsea had not said, "I told you so." Instead, her BFF whispered in her ear, "You're beyond him. You're gonna be a huge movie star." Louder, Chelsea cheered, "This is off the hook!"

"She's right," Alex agreed. "This is a very big deal. You're set to meet with Daniel in a couple of days—give you time to read and think about the script. He expects all his actors to contribute creative ideas. Listen, Kenzie, he really went to bat for you, against the advice of the producers and casting directors."

"Why?" she blurted. "All I've ever done is *Spywitness Girls*. I mean, do you guys know why he picked me?"

"Your eyes," Alex said with a shrug, like he didn't get it, either. "Daniel says they're haunted. Just like the character you'll be playing."

Kenzie couldn't hold it in. She burst out laughing. "Haunted? That's a first."

The giddy group trooped upstairs to the VIP room. Behind closed doors is where the serious celebrating happened. Rudy ordered champagne, but Alex—who knew he was such a cagey one?!—had brought something stronger. Expertly, Kenzie's dapper agent cut lines of white powder—cocaine—for each of them.

Kenzie had never done coke before, but she'd seen enough to know how. She pressed one nostril closed, brought her head down to the table, and inhaled the soft white powder.

Snap! In an instant, she felt amazing! So sharp, focused, strong. Like . . . like . . . a flat tire pumped full of air, really fast! Her thoughts were racing: *I can do this movie, and I can be great in this movie! Screw Cole. This is my life—I am an actress. I am a star. He doesn't matter. This matters. These people matter. With them on my side, nothing can hurt me. I am strong! I am invincible! I am the NEXT BIG THING!!*

CHAPTER FOUR

Kenzie Kicks It Up a Notch—or Three

It was the Monday after the wrap party, and Milo had wasted no time spreading the news: Kenzie Cross had been handpicked by hot young director Daniel Lightstorm to star in his much buzzed-about new movie, *The Chrome Hearts Club.* The pro publicist sent out press releases, called the newspapers, magazines, texted celebrity bloggers.

The word wasn't the only thing Milo sent out. The star herself would spend every hour of the next ten days promoting the movie and herself.

Kenzie wasn't complaining—not right away, anyway. It was only when Milo went over the detailed list of appearances, interviews, and photo shoots to be squeezed in before filming started that Kenzie freaked out.

How was she going to cram it all in?

"You're young, full of energy," Milo assured her. "If you start to tire, we'll get you something to rev you back up."

By "something," she did not mean Red Bull, coffee, Pepsi, or chocolate.

As Kenzie's publicist, it was Milo's job to ensure positive publicity for the starlet. The public should see Kenzie at charity events, meeting fans, looking chic, trendy, age-appropriate, wholesome, and happy, whether out for a shopping spree, red carpet premiere, or lunch date.

Alternately, the public should not see underage drinking, partying too hard, or any other pre-rehab Lohan-slash-Spears-ian escapades.

Kenzie hadn't always made that last bit easy, but Milo had proved a pro at covering up, or casting reasonable doubt on any unsavory gossip.

Now, the starlet was made aware, the rules were different. "More teen magazine and fashion covers, fewer tabloid headlines, sweetie pie," as Rudy had gently put it. The movie had catapulted her into a different league and she had to adjust accordingly.

First stop on the "Kenzie-Go-Round," as she and Chelsea dubbed the following days, was a PSA, or Public Service Announcement. Kenzie had seen many of them on TV. It'd be a snap to do this one.

Dressed in a casual V-necked T-shirt and jeans, her hair falling loosely around her shoulders, Kenzie gave the camera a friendly, caring smile and read the words on the teleprompter.

"What's up, everyone? I'm Kenzie Cross and I'm here to talk about a very serious subject: texting and driving.

"Most of you know me as Morgan from *Spywitness Girls*. My real life is exciting, too. I go everywhere! But when I'm behind the wheel of my car, I never, ever, take my eyes off the road. If you're texting someone, you're not watching the road. That's when accidents happen. You could hurt yourself or even kill someone else."

She paused to let the chilling severity sink in.

"So take it from me, Kenzie Cross, text everyone you

know—when you're out of the car! And remember, don't even think about driving if you've had even one drink."

"Cut!" the director of the PSA called out. "Great job, Kenzie, we appreciate you doing this."

"Thank you for giving me the opportunity to talk to my fans about something important," she said. "If I can help save one life, it's worth it."

That wasn't total BS. Had Kenzie texted while driving back home? She hated to admit it, even to herself, but yeah. Now it was a nonissue. Either Chelsea texted for her, or they had a chauffeur.

After the PSA, Kenzie, Chelsea, and Milo were limo'd to the *Teen Vogue* studio for a photo shoot. Milo, who never met a compliment she didn't personally deserve, took major props for this one. "You're getting the *cover*. It's their fall issue, the biggest one—what a coup!"

This was not a news flash. Milo had sung this song before, how she'd talked editors out of their original cover choice, Hayden, in favor of Kenzie. Milo used the movie news as ammunition, insisting that the *Heroes* star would be old news, while Kenzie wore the next-big-thing tiara.

Kenzie wasn't a fan of that story (true or not), wasn't thrilled hearing it yet again in the limo. It felt exactly like when she got the bigger dressing room, as if she'd snatched something away from someone else.

"Hayden's a wonderful actress—and a good role model," she protested. "She's on a hit show, she sings and saves the dolphins. No way I'm a bigger star."

"Being on the cover *makes* you the bigger star," Milo responded. "The rest doesn't count."

To Hayden, it did, Kenzie was sure.

"Maybe you've got the better team working for you, Kenzie," Chelsea opined.

"Working" being the operative word. Posing for a magazine cover, Kenzie soon found, was glamorous—*and* tedious. Being pampered was the glam part; all she had to do was get comfortable, put her feet up while a pedicurist went to work, lean back over the sink so the hairdresser's assistant could give her a shampoo and scalp massage, and keep her eyes closed so the makeup artist could apply liner, eye shadow, and mascara.

Trying on clothes from the racks and racks offered was—who'da thunk it?—disappointing. The *Teen Vogue* fashion editors had their vision of what she should look like; Kenzie's personal stylist had her own, and Milo was there to "yea" or "nay" anything that wasn't right for Kenzie's wholesome-but-edgier image. Which left Kenzie herself aced out of deciding what she wanted to wear.

Some of the outfits were killer. She rocked the blue Cavalli top that match ed her eyes and craved the Prada boots she posed in. But after what felt like fifty outfits later, Kenzie understood what a mannequin must feel like (do mannequins have feelings?), trying to stand still while being dressed and redressed, pinned and posed against a set of different backgrounds.

Then there was the tedium, what actors and models call "hurry up and wait." Kenzie had to be ready, prompt, upbeat for every shot, then wait while the lights and reflector umbrellas were set and reset.

Thankfully, she had Chelsea around, and the two of them got into reading the fashion magazines that were lying around, texting their friends, taking calls. Gabe gave them a heads-up about a party at LAX that night; Lev needed advice about this new girl he was interested in.

Unfortunately, there was enough downtime for Kenzie to obsess about Cole's catting around the other night. If she hadn't been so drunk and stoned and astounded, the hurt would have hit her sooner. Sober, she felt the sting of his public betrayal.

Unsurprisingly, when Model Boy heard the big *Chrome Hearts Club* news, he tried, via voice message and texts, to convince her she hadn't seen him making out with someone else (!). When that boneheaded lie failed, Cole changed his story. He was, he swore, swapping saliva for a good cause: helping a new actress rehearse her first on-screen kiss. Which prompted Chelsea to quip, "There's a reason models have a reputation for being morons. Cole is their poster boy."

Still, it took all Kenzie's willpower not to return his calls. She'd never had boy trouble in her life, and she'd really liked being his girlfriend.

Alex had left a message, reminding her to prepare for her meeting with Daniel Lightstorm, the movie director. Waiting around would have been prime time to read the screenplay, and take her mind off Cole, only she'd left it home.

Directly after the interminable *Teen Vogue* photo shoot, Milo whisked her off to an appearance at the new Zac Posen boutique. Just for showing up and posing with the designer, she got a free shopping spree. Mostly, Chelsea did the shopping; Kenzie was truly tired of trying things on.

Milo pulled her aside and made good on her promise to "keep Kenzie's energy up." The publicist turned out to be a one-woman pharmacy. Kenzie had her choice of amphetamines.

She took two Adderall: They did the trick. Maybe a little too well.

She was upbeat and chatty during a live interview with *E!*'s Ryan Seacrest, positively sparkled on MTV and *Access Hollywood*. Kenzie's last gig of the day was an "exclusive" interview about *The Chrome Hearts Club* to *People* magazine. She raced through it, glossing over the movie details, since she didn't know any, and instead offered witty anecdotes that seemed to satisfy the reporter.

Finally, the work part of her day was over. Kenzie was far, far from fatigued. Thanks to the uppers, the starlet was wired. Going home to chill was not an option.

After dinner at celebrity hangout Dolce and a quick trip home to shower and change, Kenzie and Chelsea met up with Gabe and Lev, and made for Teddy's, an exclusive outdoor-indoor club at the Hollywood Roosevelt that Gabe was hoping to snare as a client.

She started the evening totally mindful of being discreet: *This is the first night of the rest of my life as a movie star,* she told herself. Kenzie was careful; she kept her drinking to a minimum, her dancing less steamy, her flirting nonexistent. Being on a boy-less diet seemed best.

Then Cole showed up.

Avoiding him, keeping her head high, her tears down,

and ignoring his pleas to get back together, took a chemical assist: Gabe supplied the Xanax, Lev, the Vicodin; Cole sent bottles of Patrón tequila to the table.

Which she should have sent back. But why? As long as he thought he was paying penance, she'd go ahead and enjoy herself. She downed a couple of shots.

Kenzie couldn't recall how it happened, but hours later, somehow, she found herself in the middle of a game of Flip Cup—a relay race, but with drinking.

Kenzie had played it plenty of times. Teams face each other across a table and pour beer into a cup. The first person has to tip the cup by its lid until it flips in a cartwheel, without spilling any. If he or she misses (which is, always), he or she has to drink what's in the cup. The next team doesn't go until the first person on the opposing team wins a round. A lot of beer gets consumed.

That night, Cole suggested a slightly different version: Strip Flip Cup. Whenever someone lost a round, everyone on the team had to take something off.

Kenzie couldn't deny it was more fun that way—though why she allowed herself to get into a game with sniveling creep Cole was beyond her. Still, she hadn't laughed so hard in days—and she felt safe. They played in the VIP Room, where no cameras, not even cell phones, were allowed. So even though Kenzie's team lost big-time, and no one got fully frontal, no way would any photos of her "naughty night" get out.

She shouldn't have gotten busted at all. Then Cole upped the stakes again.

Instead of a paper cup, the bronze braggart would use

a glass beer stein. He flipped it, hard. It flew into the air—backward. It was like in a movie going slo-mo. All eyes were on the heavy glass mug it as arced into the air. Only, unlike in a movie, it didn't stay suspended up there. It came crashing down. In a moment of epic bad timing, the club manager walked in. Guess what the glass crashed on?

Kenzie's crowd got tossed from the club; she barely had time to get dressed. The paparazzi were waiting to pounce.

Kenzie needed a serious caffeine and Adderall boost to get going the next morning. The day was going to be packed with meetings. But first, the Milo-scolding. Last night's romp-in-the-near-nude made the online columns, and Milo was majorly unamused.

The publicist handled it by sticking to the story that Kenzie only drank Red Bull, club soda, and water, and was merely a spectator in the rowdy game. The fact that Kenzie exited the club with her top on backward and her pants unzipped was a fashion statement. End of story.

Kenzie felt guilty, forcing Milo to have to go to such lengths to "defend" her—and solemnly swore (to herself) to not let that happen again. She'd been rattled by Cole's presence; that's what led to risky behavior. It was a new day, she was over him.

First on Kenzie's to-do list was a meeting with the Neutrogena advertisers. They were deciding on the "new face" for their campaign. Kenzie oozed sweet and wholesome charm, adding that she used Neutrogena all the time.

There were meetings about a yearly Kenzie calendar, posters, books, and a Kenzie perfume. "All the big stars have a fragrance," was Alex's reasoning. "That's crucial."

"We're thinking of calling it 'Kiss Me Kenzie,'" Rudy followed up.

Sounded like Tickle Me Elmo.

The afternoon meeting her team was most excited about was the one Kenzie found most perplexing.

"The Juicy Couture execs want you to start your own collection. Couture by Kenzie, or JCKC, you know, like DKNY. How does that strike you?" Agent Alex thought this a stroke of brilliance. On his part, since he'd thought it up.

Kenzie's protests that she couldn't design a tic-tac-toe board went unheard.

Chelsea was all over it, "She'd be a celebrity designer, like . . . Mary-Kate and Ashley? SJP? JLo?" She turned to Kenzie, wide eyed. "Oh my God, you'd be like Lauren Freakin' Conrad!! This is so amazing!"

"The line will consist of jeans, tops, and flirty dresses at first, then we'll add capris, sandals, and accessories," Alex described.

Kenzie couldn't think straight. But she did hear him loud and clear when he added, "We are looking at a serious bump in salary next season. Add up all your endorsements, and you'll make next year's Richest Celebrity lists."

How was that even possible? Being the NBT was one thing, but already she made more money in a week than her dad ever made in a year. Too bizarre. And . . . wrong somehow. He'd worked so hard, all his life. And her? Not so much.

"Multimillionaire Kenzie Cross. Has a nice ring to it, doesn't it?" Alex said with a wink and a knowing smile.

Her dad could *retire,* it hit her, she could buy him and Seth a big house. Oh, and that vacation cabin on San Juan Island he fantasized about! And a car, a truck even. Maybe Seth could go to private school—or better, join the traveling soccer team. They'd even have enough money if the team went to England to play, or anywhere, really.

There was only one way she could blow her bountiful future. Team Kenzie drummed it into her at every opportunity. They called. They texted. They e-mailed: Keep the partying under the radar. Stay on-trend. Think Miley. Think Hayden, The Jonas Brothers. *Not* anyone named after a famous hotel chain. Or Spears.

"You don't have to be a shut-in," Milo kept reminding her, "just make sure that whatever you do, there's enough reasonable doubt to be deniable."

Kenzie knew the drill: Fill a water bottle with vodka. Pop pills at private home parties or VIP rooms, go into nightclub bathroom stalls alone, leave clubs through back doors. Don't get caught. That'd been last night's mistake.

"Look, I know this is a lot," Milo said after another day of self-promotion. "Just think before you act. And remember, Wednesday is the most important day of the week. You're meeting with Daniel Lightstorm, your director. You have read the script, right?"

Wednesday. Wait . . . that day sounded familiar. She was supposed to be somewhere. "Seth's soccer game!" she blurted. "I can't do it that day."

"*Can't* is no longer part of your vocabulary, Kenzie. If you really want to be a star—a brand—not just that girl on a TV show, if you want to leverage your new movie-star status, you need to do everything we've set up for you," Alex reminded her.

"I know and I appreciate it, I really do, guys. I'm trying to keep up—I mean, I want to! But when do I get a break?"

"If we're lucky? Not in the foreseeable future." Alex was not kidding. "Not after we've put in all this work for you. We're breaking butt here, all for you. You've got to be on board. You are, aren't you?"

"Yeah. I mean, I guess."

"You can't guess. There are too many people depending on you. This is the big time, Kenzie." Alex said it, but the trio looked like bobbleheads agreeing.

CHAPTER FIVE

Elevator Going Down(hill)

Kenzie hadn't counted on feeling this way. Like suddenly she was *responsible* for all these people—Alex, Rudy, Milo, and even their assistants, now depending on her.

She'd faced pressure before. For years, after her mother had hitched up and ridden into the sunset, she'd taken care of Seth, the house, gone to school, and kept up her drama lessons, her secrets, and her popularity. That's pressure!

It'd never been a real problem. Her dad counted on her and had been proud of her. Seth worshipped her; she handled her schoolwork, had tons of friends, and a really active social life. Not once had she taken her eyes off the prize—breaking into showbiz.

During her senior year, she'd created her own webisodes on her Facebook page, where each week she enacted scenes from a movie, or crazy things that'd happened in real life: displaying her talent for drama as well as comedy. Miraculously, it made its way to YouTube, where it was flagged by Alex's assistant. She'd been flown to Los Angeles for auditions. At eighteen, fresh out of high school, she'd gotten her break.

She'd done it all. Pressure be damned.

Everything was going exactly as she dreamed it would,

just bigger and faster. She understood why she was being kept so busy, just not why everything seemed harder. Kenzie didn't like admitting this, even to herself, but she was suddenly fearful of letting people down.

Somehow, she seemed to do that at every turn. In fact, downturn was the direction the next several days took.

Milo had booked her on the morning TV shows, scheduled interviews with *Us Weekly* and *OK!* magazine, plus a bunch of online chats. It'd been bumper-to-bumper promotion, but Kenzie had been professional and gone into them revved and ready.

Her stylist had rounded up really cute outfits, and she met everyone from Vanessa Minnillo to Mark (pant, pant) McGrath. The questions they put to her were totally puffball, like always. She had no trouble fielding them.

Best of all, so she'd thought, the day she was to have met with director Daniel got rescheduled to Friday, clearing her for Seth's soccer game on Wednesday.

Kenzie was pumped! She even bought a gift for Seth: his very own Wii console, and Guitar Hero video game. She must have blabbed her plans to the salesclerk, forgetting that paparazzi pay for tips like these, because when she got to the soccer field, a dozen cameramen were already waiting.

Kenzie was in a quandary—normally, she'd have sent them packing, but mindful of Milo's instructions to be noncontroversial, compliant with the press, she posed sweetly for everyone, gave good sound bites. She wasn't going to let her team down.

Inadvertently, she let the home team down. Her dad was

not cool with his son's game being swarmed by photographers. The frenzy took everyone's focus off the field. Kenzie felt guilty but promised to make it up to both of them. As soon as she could.

The next day was suck-a-rama Thursday. It was wall-to-wall interviews with reporters on teleconference, piped in from all over the country. She had to be in a soundproof room for hours, trying to come up with good answers to their questions.

This bunch wanted actual details about *The Chrome Hearts Club*.

She knew some of it—Sarah, the name of her character, for instance—but not much else. A fact she hadn't even realized until the moment when she was asked what makes Sarah tick, why had that girl formed *the Chrome Hearts Club,* and how did Kenzie relate to her movie character? Kenzie did her best to vague it up or pretend she wasn't allowed to give out any details.

Somewhere inside, she knew she was busted. She just didn't know how busted.

So when Milo offered her a hit of cocaine so she could get through the *Seventeen* magazine fashion show benefit after the round-robin interviews, Kenzie accepted gratefully. Those non-Hollywood newshounds had worn her out and, though she didn't tell Milo, scared her!

By the end of the day, Kenzie craved party time. She had energy to burn and guilt feelings about not having read the screenplay to quell.

The antidote was one private house party and three clubs. She and her friends danced, drank, giggled, and gossiped the night away. Kenzie had her own private moment at Avalon with Logan Ford. Who just so happened to be a model, and, coincidentally, Cole Rafferty's rival.

It was at Blue Velvet where things really got out of hand.

Kenzie was minding her own business, a little wrecked, dancing with her friends, when who should show up and get in their faces, but Cole, all hot, hunky, and hammered.

"Let's motor," she'd said to Gabe when the unshaven underwear model pushed into their circle.

"I know about your little make-out session with Logan." Cole charged at her.

"Someone text-bomb you?" Kenzie quipped. How else could he have found out that quickly?

"You're a slut," he cursed at her.

Before Kenzie could react, Lev inserted himself between the exes. "No one talks to my friend that way," Lev growled.

"Bring it," Cole shot back, ready for fisticuffs.

Lev, who was more a lover than fighter, did. He shoved Cole, who hadn't expected the lean string bean to be that strong, went flying backward. The muscled model went to punch Lev, but missed.

Meanwhile, Kenzie, Gabe, and Chelsea tried to break it up before they got thrown out. Mission: not accomplished. The group was out on its collective keister.

Cole was sent packing.

Yet Kenzie was up for more. They hit Opera, where, fueled by vodka stingers and Vicodin, she danced up a storm, and even got to sing with Fall Out Boy's Pete Wentz in the deejay booth, rocking out to Blue Öyster Cult!

It was there that she spotted a waitress wearing Versace platform Mary Janes—with the sickest heels ever, like six inches. She had to have them. At least to play with. The waitress agreed to switch shoes, and Kenzie went teetering around the club in her tower-of-power shoes. Dancing was a laugh riot.

"You look like the stilt girl in the circus!" Chelsea called up to her.

"I can't hear you," she shouted down. "I look like blitz girl? I am blitzed!"

When they left, well after three A.M., the 'razzi were waiting. Stayed up all night to catch this moment. Unintentionally, Kenzie made it worth their while. She wanted to ask Gabe, who was behind her, if this club was one of his—had they brought publicity to it? Turning around was a bad move. Kenzie clumsily slipped out of the shoes. The last thing she remembered before everything went black was the sound of her tush hitting the pavement. Not a pretty sound.

CHAPTER SIX

Blackmailed into Rehab

"Tell me why you're here, Kenzie," Dr. Wanderman asked.

"Blackmail."

It was the Saturday after suck-a-rama Thursday, and Kenzie found herself in a place she never could have imagined: the earthy-cozy, flower-filled office of Dr. A. G. Wanderman, at the Serenity Lake Rehabilitation Center.

The starlet was anything but serene.

Dr. Wanderman, a small, perky woman with a halo of wild auburn hair, was the chief psychiatrist. *The head head-doctor,* Kenzie thought bitterly.

"Who blackmailed you?" she asked, leaning in a bit closer.

"Everyone! People I trusted. My *team.* They forced me to come here and no one stood up for me." Her voice cracked suddenly.

Dr. Wanderman offered a tissue. "Stood up for you about what?"

"I don't need to be here! They all betrayed me."

"You signed yourself in," she pointed out, not unkindly.

"Under great distress! Duress. It's a total mistake," Kenzie said, blowing her nose.

"Start from the beginning, Kenzie. What happened? If it is a mistake, maybe we can do something to rectify it."

Friday, the day Kenzie was to have met with Daniel Lightstorm, did not go well. In a tsunami kind of not-going-well way.

The director who'd fought to have Kenzie in his movie refused to see her.

Mostly, Kenzie would learn later that afternoon in a head-spinning conference call with Alex, Rudy, and Milo, it was because of the interviews, the ones Milo had set up so she could promote *The Chrome Hearts Club*. In Daniel's view, Kenzie had come off like some ditzy airhead during her TV appearances. Apparently, though Kenzie didn't remember saying this, when *Extra* host Mark McGrath jokingly asked her if he could join the Chrome Hearts Club, she'd said, "Sure!," forgetting the plot revolved around a group of desperate delinquents.

Okay, that was the wrong answer. She got it.

In another interview, she'd apparently made it sound like a comedy.

What really burned the director was that Kenzie hadn't even "bothered" to read the screenplay; she was a flake who cared nothing about his movie.

Kenzie begged to differ. Wasn't all that promotion *for* the movie? No one had given her time to read the screenplay or prepped her ahead of time.

There was more. An article in the *New York Post*. Alex read it to Kenzie:

"For a film with so much buzz and a sterling supporting cast, why would Daniel Lightstorm cast this town's MVP—most vapid partier—in the lead role? This reporter assumed Kenzie Cross might address that question during our interview, give some clue that she can do more than Spywitless Girls *and throw down shots at Les Deux, but in her parlance, "not even." Instead, she giggled girlishly, deflecting questions about the film, making one wonder if she'd even read the script. I know she's being touted all over town as "the next big thing," but this reporter isn't drinking the Kenzie Kool-Aid. We'll have to wait for the film to come out, but I think young Lightstorm has made the mistake of his career."'*

Kenzie was burning, enraged. For one thing, there is no deal for Kenzie Kool-Aid, just clothes, cleanser, and perfume. Before she had a chance to defend herself, Alex, Rudy, and Milo dropped the F-bomb:

Daniel was *firing* her. From the movie.

Kenzie gasped so loudly, at first she didn't hear the rest of what they were saying. No way would she ever have anticipated it. Not this.

Team Kenzie caucused, and eventually came up with a plan they could all agree on. They took it straight to the director, bypassing their client.

Kenzie, they decided, would voluntarily check herself into rehab. She'd do at least thirty days. If she cleaned up her act, would Daniel agree to hold the movie for her?

"What act?" Kenzie had demanded. "I don't have an

act. I'm just being me. The same me he fought for, 'Kenzie with the haunted eyes.'"

She refused the deal. She'd just take the summer off, do a second season of *Spywitness Girls,* move on.

"Not so fast," had been Alex's response. "Getting fired from a movie has serious consequences. The TV network will think twice about you. Advertisers don't want a nineteen-year-old sloppy drunk representing their show."

Kenzie'd protested she'd never be fired from *Spywitness Girls.* Was she not the franchise? The star? The only reason the show's a hit? Hadn't *he* specifically said so?

Alex rolled his eyes in a don't-you-know-anything way. "They'll just get another franchise. Amber and Romy are champing at the bit."

Kenzie's head was spinning. "How'd I get from talented to tainted without even passing Go?" she demanded, incensed. "Riddle me that."

"Oh, sweetie, I know it's hard, but there's no other way," Rudy said ruefully. "You'll have to adjust, but I know you can do it."

Milo's two cents: "Rehab can be a better career move than making the TV-to-movie jump."

They'd totally thought this through, wrote an entire scenario without her.

"This is how we're framing it," Milo had said. "You're not addicted to anything. In fact, this is pre-hab. You're so responsible that you realize you might be getting in over your head. So, you're getting help before it's too late. You have to agree this is a brilliant strategy."

Team Kenzie was in spin mode. They were spinning her. It wasn't going to work. She was not going into rehab.

As tears fell unbridled, Kenzie now faced Dr. Wanderman. She hadn't seen a way out. There was no way to go up against her handlers. Her friends had deserted her, agreeing with the advisors. Worst of all, her dad voted in favor of rehab.

Kenzie felt like a pawn in some bigger game, a thing to be pushed around, used. Not a person.

"You're very angry," Dr. Wanderman commented, after listening to Kenzie's blackmail story.

"No shit," she retorted. "I'm in lockdown for no reason. I'm a good person, a fun person. A few days ago, I was the person everyone wanted to be, or be with. So how'd I end up alone, without a cell phone, BlackBerry, laptop, TV, or even an iPod?" Those were the rules she'd been informed of upon check-in that morning.

"It's just for a while," the good doctor said. "In two weeks, you'll able to do e-mail or texting for an hour a day."

Big friggin' deal, she thought sourly.

"It's not punishment," Dr. Wanderman continued, "even though I know it feels like it. To expedite recovery, it's crucial to isolate all our guests from outside influences—the people who've enabled you to get in over your head—so you can concentrate on your inner self, the first step toward sobriety."

"I am sober! I don't need to be isolated," Kenzie groused, wishing she had a Xanax or Vicodin to mellow her out.

Dr. Wanderman flipped through a file, obviously Kenzie's.

"It says here you blacked out a few days ago. Was that from too much drinking?"

She must be referring to Thursday night, Kenzie concluded. "No. I fell because of the stupid shoes. I was pushing my luck and it ran out. I hit the pavement and blacked out, but only for a moment."

"But you had been drinking, right? And then you lost consciousness," the doctor persisted.

"You say it like it's a bad thing," Kenzie complained, "or something that hasn't been captured by a zillion paparazzi before. No one ever mentioned rehab to me—not my agent, manager, Milo, my friends—and suddenly, wham! They blackmail me into it."

Dr. Wandeman pursed her lips. "So you were doing what you always do, only this time, you got coerced, forced, into coming here. Is that how you see it, Kenzie?"

"Exactly." Kenzie's tears had dried, crusted on her face, which she obstinately refused to wipe away. She was over this "intake" session; beyond ready to leave. To go home.

Not an option.

"I'd like to ask about your family history," Dr. Wanderman said.

"Go for it," Kenzie grumbled, squirming.

"Is there a history of addiction in your family?" she asked.

"Sure," Kenzie quipped. "My dad's a carpenter, he's addicted to supporting his family. My brother's ten, a total soccer addict."

Ignoring Kenzie's sarcasm, Dr. Wanderman continued, "And your mom?"

"Out of the picture."

"I'm sorry, did she pass on?" the doctor inquired.

"Passed through is more like it. She skipped out after Seth was born."

Dr. Wanderman found this fact intriguing, Kenzie was hardly surprised to notice.

"Look," Kenzie said, before the inevitable drilling began, "I know you think it's some big trauma. Guess what, it isn't. We've been doing just fine, better than fine. My dad's an amazing man. He's everything—"

She broke off, unable to continue. For her dad had betrayed her too, hadn't he? Told her he'd been worried about her, but Kenzie hadn't taken his concerns seriously, insisting that he "just didn't understand" what it took to be a star. At this point, he believed rehab was in her best interest.

Kenzie had tried to make him understand that this was all about the movie—that's all anyone cared about, appeasing the director. Her dad wouldn't listen. He said all he cared about—all he'd ever cared about—was her health and well-being. He questioned how much Kenzie cared about that.

She was full-out sobbing now.

Dr. Wanderman was sympathetic. "I can see why you believe you were manipulated into coming here, Kenzie. Frankly, I think you're lucky."

Frankly, my doc, I don't give a damn what you think. I am screwed.

CHAPTER SEVEN

—SIMON & GARFUNKEL, "MRS. ROBINSON"

Kenzie was floating, lazily making snow angels on a poufy cloud, drifting aimlessly in the sky. The pristine white cloud embraced her, kept her safe, protected—yet unconstrained, free. She was anchored, and flying; she had weight, but felt so light, airy. A soft breeze carried her along.

Kenzie flipped over on her tummy as she knew she was supposed to, so she could see her, the woman on horseback. Her silky long blond hair was caught in a ponytail, which swung from side to side, as she trotted along. The woman looked familiar, but Kenzie couldn't place her. She was riding away from her. Kenzie descended almost close enough to see her face. But just as Kenzie got near, the woman turned, peered over her shoulder, disappeared in a blur.

As recurring dreams go, hers was not that bad, Kenzie told herself, as she awoke, anxious and sweaty after her first night in rehab. Not that she'd had this one in a long time. It took a few minutes to shake off the unsettling mood the dream always left her in, to force herself into consciousness. The readout on the Bose alarm clock/radio said 6:00 A.M.; gentle strains of new-age music were being piped into her room. Must be the daily "wake-up" call. Rehab reveille.

She turned to gaze at the first pink rays of dawn filtering through the gauzy curtains, defusing mistily across her nightstand.

Kenzie considered her options. She could pick her head up off the fluffy down pillows that must have played the role of clouds in her dream, rouse herself from the heavenly king-size bed, and officially start her rehab sentence. Or not.

Before she'd left Dr. Wanderman's office yesterday, she'd been given a daily schedule, which she'd tossed on the night table. Now, she reached out to consult it. She was supposed to take a daily meditative walk around the lake at six thirty A.M.

What did she have to meditate about? Spending thirty days here? Her brain would curl up into a fetal position and shut off.

She turned over, put the pillows over her head, and went back to sleep.

The next thing she heard was an annoying, persistent knock on the door.

Ignoring it was not helpful. A key turned, followed by the unmistakable sound of someone entering the room. Instantly, Kenzie was overcome by the mouthwatering aroma of fresh-brewed coffee and just-baked bread.

"Time to rise and shine, sleepyhead," chirped a crisply dressed staffer, palming a food-filled tray. "I'm Emily, and I'll be your nutrition counselor during your stay here. Since you didn't make it to the dining room, I brought breakfast to you."

"Go away, I'm not hungry." Kenzie wished she could drum up a pouty grouse, but her stomach had other plans.

It growled. She settled for sarcasm. "Is breakfast in bed something all the inmates get?"

"Only the special ones," Emily said with a wink, placing the tray on the nightstand. "But it's really more fun to eat in the dining room with your fellow inmates. Try it later, and we'll go over your customized meal plan."

Before Emily was out the door, the corners of Kenzie's mouth were flecked with croissant crumbs. She speared a chunk of fresh cantaloupe, well on her way to devouring the entire fresh fruit salad and carafe of coffee.

If that was a ruse to get her out of bed, she thought, score one for their side.

She headed for the shower. The sumptuous spa-bathroom was pretty awesome, decorated in soothing shades of blue marble and tile. Heated floors, even. She'd seen bathrooms with Jacuzzis before—had even frolicked in a couple—but the six showerheads, aiming water at all body parts, was a first.

As a rising star, Kenzie couldn't personally afford this kind of luxury. She made a mental note: *after having risen?* She was so hiring a decorator to copy this bathroom. Not just for herself. In Dad's new house, which so far existed only in her imagination, there'd be another just like it.

A plunging sadness gripped her. She was banned from calling home. She wouldn't know if Seth liked the Wii she'd sent or how the soccer season was going. Or how he'd done on the math test he'd been stressing about. Rehab, Kenzie concluded, was worse than jail. Being incarcerated, she'd be able to talk to her family on a phone through a glass partition.

She dabbed her tears with a huge Egyptian cotton towel: She'd stock up on these in her fantasy bathroom too. She considered going back to bed, but by this time, was not the least bit tired.

She *could* start a journal. Serenity Lake suggested journaling as a way to get her real feelings out.

What would she write? That she needed a Xanax; she'd like a drink—and by the way: She wanted OUT of here! Kenzie knew that already, didn't need to write it down.

Her eyes fell on the sad-looking duffel bag she'd stashed by the walk-in closet. Inmates . . . that is, guests . . . were allowed to bring one small item of luggage. It was supposed to hold everything you'd need for recovery. Somehow, Chelsea, or Milo maybe, had managed to find room for *The Chrome Hearts Club* screenplay. Kenzie considered pulling it out, starting it.

Then reconsidered.

She returned to the Serenity Lake guest schedule. Every hour of every day was accounted for. After the meditative walk around the lake at dawn, her choices included swimming, hiking, group therapy, crafting, tennis, equine therapy, yoga, and recovery work. It read like a really expensive summer camp for addicts.

Kenzie was not an addict; there was nothing to recover from. She tossed the schedule on the plushly carpeted floor. She felt jittery, so she decided to leave her gilded cage of a room. She peeked out the sliding doors, which opened onto a patio, facing the main grounds.

She withdrew a pair of loose-fitting cargoes, a shapeless black top, and pink-sequined Kate Spade ballet shoes, caught her hair up in a claw clip, and put on a pair of trendy oversize sunglasses those nice people at D&G had sent over.

She checked the mirror: Mary-Kate on a Starbucks run stared back at her. Except without the huge bag and latte.

Kenzie slipped outside, instinctively scoping the area. Were paparazzi lurking? She sighed. Probably not so much.

She wandered aimlessly, ending up on a flagstone path. Following it seemed the path of least resistance. It took her by the villas, a dozen or so, identical to hers. Each was two stories tall, had arched windows, patios, or Juliet balconies and orangey-red Spanish-tile roofs. They formed a horseshoe shape around the main grounds, or campus, as it was cheerily referred to.

The grounds did remind her of a college campus—or a lush, green country club without golf carts or a bar. The huge grassy über-landscaped quadrangle was covered with a manicured lawn, sculpted shrubs, and colorful flower gardens. The quad was dotted with shady palm, citrus, and oak trees, under which various rehabbers were reading, meditating, munching, doing yoga, chatting.

Joining any of them was beyond Kenzie's current capacity. She stuck to the path, skirted the perimeter. With each step, she felt smaller, invisible almost, sorry for herself. In a lame attempt to cheer herself up, she tried to scope out a celebri-habber to maybe approach, but she recognized no one.

A clutch of people sitting cross-legged in a circle caught her eye—not because there was a star among them, just that they were young, toned, good-looking. Like Kenzie's own circle of friends, minus the drinks, dancing, or drugs, and the sitting in a circle thing. Another pang of loneliness socked her in the gut like a speeding fastball.

Kenzie hated being alone. Everyone knew that! Where were they now? She plowed on, oblivious to where she was headed, remembering Friday night's conversation with her friends. They'd all come to her apartment for a "going away" party, to raise Kenzie's spirits, make her see that rehab wasn't the worst thing that could happen. Gabe's idea.

Her club promoter pal had even declared—martini in hand—"everyone who's anyone does rehab." Then he babbled on about the trendy booze-alert anklet she'd probably get to wear afterward. Like that was some kind of prize accessory. After a few more drinks, Gabe expansively proclaimed that thanks to Kenzie Cross, pre-hab will totally be the new black.

Chelsea urged Kenzie to put her mad acting skills to good use (yeah, Chels hadn't been exactly sober that last night). "Think of it as if you're researching a role," Chelsea had advised. "While inside, relax and enjoy. It'll be just like a super-spa," she'd declared, "with around-the-clock pampering, massages, manicures, facials, hairdressers, makeup artists." Chelsea was pretty sure there'd be all-access in-'n'-out passes and plenty of celebrity company. Chelsea made it sound as if Kenzie had just won an all-expenses-paid vacation to paradise.

That vision did little to console Kenzie.

Lev's reaction had surprised her. He promised Kenzie the whole thing would be like a cakewalk—except for having to sneak booze, weed, pills, what-have-you. Something about his matter-of-factness made Kenzie quiz him about his vast knowledge of rehab.

That's when Lev let loose a stunner. He'd been to Serenity

Lake many times—as a visitor. Turned out Lev had a sister. A twin sister, to be precise. Maxie was her name, and she was currently on her fourth stint at Serenity.

"Why?" would have been the obvious question. But the ones that came out of Kenzie were, "You have a twin? And I didn't know that, why?"

Kenzie's walk was taking her away from the main campus. She found herself wondering if she'd recognize Lev's twin sister. Had she noticed anyone tall, slim—gangly maybe?— with Lev's casual, loping gait? She actively watched for a Lev-ette with light brown hair, sparkling blue eyes— completely whacked-out. She realized that lots of guests actually fit that description. Had she walked right by Lev's trippy sister without realizing it?

Kenzie continued to follow the path. The farther away from campus it got, the more isolated she felt. Furtively, she wondered if she'd stumble across an exit—and escape! As if.

Her path led, instead, to an area dense with trees. In spots, their branches and leaves formed canopies, which was kinda pretty. Something else she noted: The farther away from campus she got, the less precious the environment, and the fresher the air.

Made sense. Serenity Lake was in the hills of Santa Barbara, not far north of L.A., but enough so there's no smog. The fresh air reminded her of home, leading to another pang of sadness. The part of Seattle Kenzie and her family called home was actually a suburb, set directly on the Puget Sound.

Ruefully, she realized she'd been in Los Angeles so long

that she had nearly forgotten what clean, pristine, ocean-tinged air smelled like.

She didn't see or hear anything at first, but Kenzie sensed she was approaching a body of water. Had to be the lake, she realized—Serenity Lake. She hiked through a patch of wildflowers, made her way up a rise. At the crest, she peered down, and there it was.

It was serene, all right. Calm, quiet, except for the easy breezes and chirping birds, peaceful. Perfect for those early morning meditative walks.

Kenzie felt lonelier than ever.

Just as she turned to leave, out of the corner of her eye she noticed a familiar pattern in the water: concentric circles rippling on the lake's surface. Like someone had tossed a stone skittering across the water.

Someone had.

He was on his haunches, just by the shore. Quietly, Kenzie watched him continue to send pebbles skimming.

Intrigued, she snuck a little closer and observed: He had thick, longish, curly hair, ropy biceps. He was wearing lived-in, butt-cupping jeans, tough-boy boots, and a rumpled, sleeveless black T-shirt.

He was alone. Forlorn, maybe? Like her? What were the chances?

Cautiously, Kenzie edged down the grass toward him. He sent more pebbles flying; he did not turn around. She came up behind him and deliberately coughed to make her presence known.

Still no reaction. Was he hard-of-hearing? Or in some rehab-related Zen state of repose?

"Hi," Kenzie said softly, tapping his shoulder. It was broad, tense to the touch.

He twisted around: Her breath caught. She'd never seen anyone with eyes that color, or colorless, before. They were wolf pale eyes, rimmed with long, thick charcoal lashes. His light-brown curly hair fell forward, covering his brow. His lips were set in a tight straight line. Unsmiling. Unfriendly.

Kenzie removed her sunglasses and stumbled ahead. "I'm new here. I was just wandering, ended up at the lake. . . ." She trailed off, realizing she was not even chipping away at his icy facade.

Au contraire: His eyelashes flickered with defiance.

Smart move: *Back away, Kenzie. Now. Who knows what kind of nutcase he is?*

Move Kenzie made: "Want company?"

His face hardened. "No."

He kind of spat that out. Well, at least he was being honest, Kenzie thought. *Guess we're not in Tinseltown anymore, Toto,* she said to herself.

The boy turned his back to Kenzie, who stood rooted to the spot.

"Don't bother, he's out of your league." A sharp, sarcastic voice broke the standoff.

Kenzie jumped. She hadn't heard anyone coming.

She spun around to find a petite, canny-eyed Asian girl whose choppy black hair looked like she'd cut it herself with a butter knife. It was a *look*, granted. It meshed with her barbed wire tattoo choker, multiple-studded leather wristbands, gobs of eyeliner, and black nail polish.

Not a Serenity Lake staffer, Kenzie concluded.

"How do you know what league I'm in?" Kenzie challenged.

"You're strictly minor league, like all the clueless celebrities who come here. He, on the other hand"—she pointed at the stone-skiffer's back—"is hard core."

"He looks pretty harmless to me," Kenzie lied.

The girl laughed. "Jeremy's got that that 'do me, I'm sensitive vibe,' but don't let it fool ya. He's a rage-aholic junkie, and he's trouble."

"How do you know so much?" Kenzie asked.

"I make it my business to know other people's sagas," the girl said, matter-of-factly.

"What's yours?" Kenzie asked.

"Just your run-of-the-mill repeat offender. Substance abuse, in all its glorious varieties," she said with a shrug.

"Were you following me?" It just then occurred to Kenzie to ask.

"Following *orders*," she clarified. "My brother, Lev, said to look after you."

A beat. Then two beats went by. Kenzie's mouth hung open. She stared stupidly, then blinked.

"I'm Maxie Romano."

CHAPTER EIGHT

A Stoned Soul Sister

"I'm guessing Lev forgot to mention that his twin sister is Chinese. Adopted, obviously. Lev loves messing with people." Maxie's eyes twinkled mischievously.

"He did say you . . . you . . . come here often," Kenzie stuttered lamely.

Thankfully, Maxie laughed. "Got that right. This makes my fourth trip here."

"Does that mean the cure rate isn't very high?" Kenzie postulated.

"Not necessarily. I like it here: It's a retreat from the hard, cold world."

Huh? If she was Lev's sister, she was the daughter of world-famous, wealthy opera singers—Lev didn't mention them much, they traveled a lot. Maxie probably lived in a mansion staffed with servants, same as Lev did, had freedom, friends, and unlimited funds to squander and enjoy. Kenzie was having trouble picturing the "hard, cold world" part.

"Want the grand tour of your new home away from home?" Maxie offered.

With a glance back over her shoulder—Hottie-by-the-Lake gave no signal he'd heard the conversation—Kenzie followed her. Maxine. Maxie.

Back on the main campus, Maxie pointed out what Kenzie had missed, the craftily camouflaged security cameras posted in the trees, shrubs, and lampposts. "Big therapist is always watching," she warned.

The girls walked around to the other side of the villas, which looked like a picture postcard of a plush resort, including tennis courts, a fitness center and spa in their own architecturally awesome building. The hundreds of acres Serenity Lake owned also housed horse stables, a yoga studio, and, at its highest point, a meditation garden.

They circled the sparkling blue lap pool, ringed by cushioned chaise longues, tables, sun umbrellas, and private cabanas with flowing white gauze curtains around them.

"The cabanas are where the hookups happen," Maxie informed her. "But there's no hanky-panky in the pool—it's staffed with two lifeguards. No one's drowning on their watch," she said. "And the villas, for residents like us—none taller than two stories. Makes it hard for the jumpers to get the job done."

"Drowning? Jumpers?" Had Kenzie heard that correctly?

"Suicides. Bad for business," Maxie said glibly. "We've got a lot of depressed guests here."

"That boy, Jeremy? By the lake. He's there without supervision."

Maxie laughed. "The lake isn't very deep, and spy-cams are everywhere. Besides, Jeremy Haven is not a flight risk. Nor is he about to off himself."

Kenzie considered. "You called him a rage-aholic. Isn't rage just depression turned outward?"

"Ooh, starlet knows her mental cases." Maxie gave her an approving nod. "Color me impressed."

"Don't be. I took intro to psych in high school to get out of calculus. Hardly makes me an expert."

"You will be when you leave here," Maxie snickered. "Serenity Lake's a jar of mixed nuts, raw and organic, salty, roasted, and totally toasted."

Ha! Maxie sounded totally normal. Funny, friendly, seemingly sober, cute in a goth way. She didn't seem nuts at all. Maybe it's true that she just likes living here, and her parents can easily afford it, and allow it.

"So where are you, Villa Primrose?" she asked, heading toward the residences.

"How'd you know?"

"That's where the special patients go. Not as in short-bus special," she amended, "as in celebrities."

When they entered the villa, Kenzie stopped halfway down the hallway. A pitifully thin woman was sitting on the floor, clinging to the plush terrycloth bathrobe she'd wrapped around herself. She was shivering and sweating at the same time. She looked familiar, but Kenzie couldn't place her. She was, however, caught by this woman's eyes: *They* were truly haunted.

"Shouldn't we call a nurse?" Kenzie called to Maxie, who'd not broken stride.

Maxie flipped around and tilted her head sympathetically. "Oh, that's Sherry, she's really not supposed to be here. There's a different wing for guests who are detoxing. I guess Sherry wandered back home."

"Should we get someone to escort her back?" Kenzie felt so horrible for this Sherry person.

"No, just leave her, poor thing. Being here is probably comforting, and she needs that as much as the detox drugs," Maxie continued down the hallway.

"I thought detoxing meant they gave you substitute drugs," Kenzie said, catching up with Maxie, "so you don't have to go through the shakes, like she is."

"Depends what you're detoxing from," Maxie said knowledgeably.

As Kenzie led Maxie into her posh quarters, she was about to ask how long detox lasted, why Sherry looked familiar, and why the woman thought of Villa Primrose as home.

Only Lev's sister was occupied. So Kenzie's first question was, "What are you doing?"

Maxie'd moved the nightstand about a foot away from the bed, and was now sitting cross-legged on the floor, squished between the bed and table. In answer to Kenzie's inquiry, Maxie pointed at the light fixture in the corner of the ceiling.

"There are cameras here, too?" Kenzie was now officially skeeved out.

"Most suicides happen in patients' rooms. You need to know how to adjust the angle, or where the blind spots are."

No need to ask why Maxie was evading the spy-cam. She reached into a small pocket sewn into the inside of her top and withdrew two little white pills.

"Wow!" Kenzie's eyes lit up. "Is that what I think it is?"

"I don't usually share my toys," she said wickedly, "but

I'll make an exception for a friend of Lev's." She paused, "Only if you want, that is."

Oh, Kenzie totally wanted. Had craved (not in an addiction kind of way, more of an "if it's there, I want it!" way) a mood enhancer since she'd arrived. Wanted it more than she'd thought she would. The sight of detox Sherry in the hallway had freaked her out. Maxie's magic pills were OxyContin, a powerful, feel-good prescription painkiller.

"How'd you get this?" Kenzie whispered, positioning herself near Maxie.

"Ah, if I told you, that'd make you complicit. We don't want our innocent little starlet to know too much, do we?"

Is she mocking me? Do I care? Not as long as there's more where that came from, Kenzie concluded.

"What about drug screenings?" Kenzie suddenly wondered, swallowing the pill quickly.

"Serenity Lake won't bother you; you're royalty. As for me? What are they going to do, make me stay longer?"

They both laughed. In that instant, Kenzie felt a weight lift, and it wasn't just the pill.

"So wait, you're saying that celebrities are really treated differently here? They don't have to submit to drug tests?"

"That's exactly what I'm sayin' sista," Maxie quipped. "The likes of you don't have to do anything you don't want to. No recovery work necessary. If you want, you can take a pass on all that stuff on your schedule. You probably wouldn't want to miss out on the manicures, massages, and gourmet meals though. They rock."

Was Maxie for real? If so, wasn't that kind of . . . defeating the purpose? Deciding to take Maxie at her word, Kenzie curled up in the comfy club chair. Maxie, meanwhile, no longer having to hide from the camera, plopped on the bed, and proceeded to give Kenzie a tutorial in Rehab 101.

She knew all the rules: No drugs, no liquor, no contact with the outside world for the first two weeks, no leaving the premises, no sex.

She also knew how to break every one.

"It's like an exclusive private high school, cliques and all," she said later on. "The popular crowd, the jocks, brainiacs, geeks, drama nerds, therapist suck-ups. The only difference is everyone's certifiable here."

"Who gets to be prom king and queen?" Kenzie giggled.

"The exercise bulimics are at the top rung of the ladder, because they're multitasking loonies. Then come the all the other eating-disorder types and the sex addicts. Alcoholics are the charmers, the druggies are into soliloquies, they'll talk your ear off. Depressives and rage-aholics, like your new friend Jeremy, are so dime a dozen, they're near the bottom of the popularity ladder. The suicidals are in their own category."

The oxy was starting to kick in. In a really lovely way.

"That detoxer, Sherry, what's she?" Kenzie asked.

"A hopeless burnout. In high school, she'd have a big *L* on her forehead, for Loser."

"What are you?" Kenzie was fascinated.

"A rebel."

"Who's in your clique?"

"Just me. So far." She eyed Kenzie . . . hopefully?

Kenzie's smile lit up the room. She'd made her first friend.

CHAPTER NINE

"Remind me why we're going to group therapy," Kenzie challenged Maxie. It was her third day in rehab. So far she'd not participated in any suggested recovery therapy. Why was Maxie shlepping her to this one?

She directed her question to Maxie's back: Kenzie followed Lev's sister up a steep trail to Serenity Lake's meditation garden.

"Group therapy is the best show in town," Maxie replied in a "you'll see" tone. "It's a total trip."

Half-credit. The *trip* was worthy. They'd climbed to the highest point on the grounds, and the view was amazing. It swept over rolling hills, the town of Santa Barbara itself, all the way out to the teal-blue ocean to the south.

That alone made the vibe completely different than on Serenity's main campus, with its sculptured shrubs and matchy-matchy flower gardens. Up here was a Zen oasis. Wildflowers grew this way and that, sprinkled with thorny roses and Spanish lavender. Kenzie inhaled, filled her lungs with the combined aroma, sweet and strong.

Seven cushioned lawn chairs were arranged in a small circle under the shade of a fig tree, a little way from where Kenzie stood. Tea service, with a plate of fresh-baked cookies, sat on a silver serving cart off to the side.

Dr. Wanderman, whose springy auburn hair was tied back in a ponytail, sat cross-legged in one of the chairs.

Three other people were there, too.

A reed-thin girl wearing a sour expression and heavy plaster casts on her legs caught Kenzie's eye immediately. How had she hiked up here? Then Kenzie noticed the wheelchair folded next to her. The girl looked away when she caught Kenzie staring at her.

A husky, scary-looking guy with close-set eyes and batwing eyebrows sat next to her. He gave Kenzie the once-over, scornfully.

Not feeling the love so far.

Then, a sweet-looking girl whose long brown hair was caught up in a side ponytail moved over to the guy, motioning that Maxie and Kenzie could sit next to each other. She must have been sweating in that long-sleeved turtlenecked top, Kenzie thought.

Dr. Wanderman took a drag of her cigarette and consulted her watch. "Most of us are here. So let's get started. First, I want to welcome Kenzie to our group. She's new to Serenity."

"Hi, Kenzie," the burly guy with the batwing eyebrows sneered. "We're honored by the presence of an actual movie star. We must be the A-list therapy group now. Where's your entourage, anyway?"

Kenzie, who'd assumed group therapy might be a gentle place, shrunk back in her chair, but Maxie got in his face. "Cut the crap, Doug. If you can't handle Kenzie being here, how 'bout you leave?"

"How 'bout the movie star takes off her dark glasses?"

Doug mimicked Maxie. "She can see us, but we can't see her?"

Dr. Wanderman intervened. "Let's introduce ourselves, and then we'll address any issues."

"Hi, I'm Jenny, a recovering anorexic. Welcome to Serenity," the smiley girl piped up.

"Didn't you leave something out?" Doug said to Jenny. "You're also a cutter. There are probably paparazzi hiding in the trees—we wouldn't want the tabloids to omit that. They're all over beautiful girls who self-mutilate."

That's why she's in long sleeves, Kenzie instantly realized. *She's ashamed. That must suck.*

"Doug," Dr. Wanderman directed, "lose the sarcasm and introduce yourself."

"Whatever. I'm Doug, and I'm here for—"

"Anger issues?" Kenzie couldn't help herself. "Paranoia?"

"Alcoholism," Doug grunted, folding his arms across his chest again. "And just because a person is paranoid doesn't mean he's not being watched."

Dr. Wanderman nodded to the girl with the casts covering her shins.

She was staring at the ground, her long dark bangs obscured her face. "My name is Hannah," she mumbled. "My legs are not broken. The casts are to break my spirit."

Kenzie's hand flew to her mouth to cover the gasp. She couldn't believe what she was hearing.

"Hannah's an exercise bulimic," Maxie explained without sarcasm. "The casts prevent her from running, swimming, or any kind of cardio, so she won't keep losing weight. It's like detox."

No, it's like being chained to a chair—like a prisoner or slave. Kenzie pictured it like medieval torture. Torture, she reminded herself, that Hannah, or her family, paid a lot of money for.

"Cast therapy seems cruel," Dr. Wanderman interjected, "but as Hannah makes further strides in her recovery, they'll come off."

Further strides? You'd think a shrink would find a better word choice, Kenzie inwardly castigated the doctor.

"Rehab," Dr. Wanderman explained as if she were reading Kenzie's mind, "isn't about punishment. It's about healing. It's about hope and joy, and remembering who you used to be, before you got sick."

Kenzie scoped the circle. Except for Jenny, who seemed a little too chipper, not a lot of joy represented.

"There you are, Jeremy." Dr. Wanderman's attention turned to a boy who'd just climbed up the hill.

Jeremy? Lake Boy Jeremy?

Kenzie twisted around. Indeed it was he, rocking the same black T-shirt, faded jeans, and—when he caught sight of Kenzie—scornful expression as he had on her first day.

"Sorry," he mumbled, grabbing the last seat, inching it outside the circle.

Kenzie wondered why Maxie hadn't mentioned Jeremy being part of the group.

Dr. Wanderman made the introductions. Jeremy, just as Maxie had said, admitted he was here to treat his drug dependency.

As if they'd been cued, all eyes turned to Kenzie. Beads

of sweat formed on her forehead. No assistants came forward to wipe them away this time.

"So what's your addiction, starlet?" Doug challenged. "Besides publicity?"

A mirthful laugh escaped. "Believe me, I am so not here for publicity. My people are working to keep this out of the news."

"I'll just bet," Doug mumbled, twisting in his chair, searching furtively for phantom paparazzi. "Your people are probably broadcasting this meeting on YouTube."

"Do you have so-called low self-esteem, like the rest of us?" This from Hannah, who'd finally looked up, pinning Kenzie with a hopeful stare.

Kenzie swallowed. When Maxie had said group therapy was the "best show in town," she'd sort of assumed she'd be a spectator. Not a participant.

"Were you dragged to Serenity Lake, like me?" Hannah again, searching Kenzie's face pleadingly.

More like pushed, she thought bitterly. Not that she'd admit the blackmail and betrayal to these strangers—ever.

Maxie, intuiting Kenzie's discomfort, broke in. "Listen, guys, I kind of convinced Kenzie to come to group therapy today. Maybe we save the home version of 'Guess My Addiction' for another session."

Dr. Wanderman agreed with Maxie, but Jenny and Hannah put in one more try.

"Are you here because you're partying too much, like all the stars?" Jenny guessed.

"You're a substance abuser," Hannah decided.

"Are you high now?" Jeremy leaned forward in his chair.

Taken aback by the accusatory tone, Kenzie retorted, "Of course not!" Unless he had X-ray vision, she assured herself, he was sitting too far away to see the effects of today's dose of painkiller, even though she'd complied and removed the shades.

"I sense resentment directed at Kenzie," Dr. Wanderman said. "It isn't helpful to her—or to any of you. Let's do a regular meeting. Hannah, would you like to go first?

A regular meeting, Kenzie quickly found out, was basically a chat fest. Each person gets to talk about whatever's on his or her mind. The hope being that therapy patients can relate to one another, commiserate, empathize, and eventually, find strength to overcome their addictions.

"What are you feeling right now?" Dr. Wanderman prompted Hannah.

"Like a prisoner being tortured. I can't move, and they try and force me to eat." Hannah's voice trembled. "I'll be an elephant by the time I leave here."

"You understand that's not rational," Dr. Wanderman said warmly. "You have an illness, and you're here to understand the reasons behind your self-destructive behavior and get better."

"What is exercise bulimia, anyway?" Kenzie heard herself ask.

Hannah wrapped her birdlike arms around herself, but didn't answer.

"Oh, go on, tell her," Doug goaded. "Maybe she'll play you in a Lifetime TV movie or something."

Could this guy be any more obnoxious? Kenzie stared daggers at him. Hannah decided to answer. "It's not as bad as anorexia," she said, turning to Jenny, "and it's not really bulimia. It's not even an eating disorder."

"Yes, it is," challenged Jenny. "That's why you're here."

"I eat! I just keep track of how many calories I take in and try to burn off at least that amount by running or swimming, or by using the elliptical machine or treadmill. It's not that big of a deal. It's cruel to do this to me," Hannah whimpered.

Kenzie's heart clutched. The use of heavy plaster casts must have been a last resort.

"Sufferers use exercise as their form of purging," Dr. Wanderman explained. "They do it more and more, and it becomes their drug. They plan their lives around their workouts. And if they can't exercise, they experience withdrawal symptoms, depression, and anxiety."

"I hope you get the casts off soon," was the best Kenzie could manage.

"Jeremy, would you like to go next?" Dr. Wanderman asked. "How are you doing?"

"Fine," he said, tipping the chair back now. "I made it through detox. Now I'm just . . . going from day to day, I guess."

"Are you going to NA meetings?" she asked.

"Not yet. I will," he said, not very convincingly.

Kenzie was dying to ask Maxie what Jeremy's exact saga was. He didn't sound like a rage-aholic. Not compared to Doug, anyway.

The biggest shock came when Doug talked. He'd spoken to his mother earlier and the conversation left him fuming. "You know what the bitch said to me? She goes, 'It's not my fault you drink, I treated you like a human being, not the evolutionary mishap you are.'"

For the second time in an hour, Kenzie tried to cover up her gasp. She refused to believe any parent would talk to her child—her son—like that. It couldn't be real. Even if Dr. Wanderman treated it seriously.

"Doug, you know she's toxic, a sick woman. She took it out on you. *You* don't need to take it out on you," the doctor reminded him.

Most likely embarrassed by his humiliating admission, Doug turned his fury on Kenzie. "Okay, TV star. We've shown you ours. It's on you now. What is your real trauma?"

"I'm sorry," Kenzie said softly. "I just don't think I belong here."

After group, Maxie suggested they hit the spa for massages and pampering. "You need it, after that grilling," she said.

"A head's-up that they were going to attack me might've been nice," Kenzie said.

"That was my brain on drugs," she giggled. "Sometimes I forget things."

Was Maxie playing her? Or had she just not thought through Doug's anger issues, or that Hannah's and Jenny's neediness might be directed at her?

Kenzie couldn't be sure, but was willing to give Maxie the benefit of the doubt when the savvy sprite invited her to share in a pre-spa relaxing ritual.

Maxie had a stash of airline-sized bottles of liquor hidden inside the springs of her mattress. The hiding spot was pretty ingenious, and the two little swigs of vodka went down very smoothly.

"So about Jeremy," Kenzie mused, rolling the tiny bottle between her thumb and forefinger.

"Him again? Trust me. He's not the bad boy of your freakish dreams," Maxie said.

"What, you think I'm into him? Not even close. I'm taking a hiatus from boys right now, anyway."

"You expect me to believe that?" Maxie said. "You're a hottie-magnet."

"I'm repelling them right now," Kenzie insisted, wondering if Maxie knew about the Cole debacle. Had Lev told her?

She threw back another swig of vodka and decided it didn't matter. Cole couldn't hurt her anymore. She was over him. Besides, she'd gotten her revenge with his rival that night at Teddy's.

"Anyway," Kenzie continued, "if I were interested in anybody, it would not be Jeremy Haven. Clearly, he can't stand the sight of me."

"Which just makes him a challenge," Maxie noted. "But from what I know, he hasn't had it easy. Sucky childhood, ended up in foster care. From there it wasn't a big leap to drugs."

"How long has he been at Serenity Lake?" Kenzie asked.

"Maybe six weeks or so? He's done with detox, and I think he's doing a lot of one-on-one recovery work with a counselor, plus other things like horseback riding, wall climbing, stuff like that," she said, doing a shot of rum.

Kenzie had counted: Maxie had downed about four little bottles in just a couple of moments. "I know we don't know each other very well, and you like to joke around—but what's your saga, really?"

"My saga? You mean, why do I drink and self-medicate? Why am I here?" Maxie asked with a sly grin.

Kenzie asked, "Have you done detox?"

"No. But that's because I don't want to detox. Being high feels better than being sober, that's all. Being high means I don't have to deal with all the family crap. I can be a frail little failure. It's easier."

Maxie didn't give Kenzie a chance to ask what, exactly, she'd failed at. Lev's little sis did a sharp convo U-turn, describing the amazing mani-pedis offered at the spa. "After your massage, you should treat yourself," she said. "It's all paid for, anyway."

"Speaking of paid for, how can our foster kid, Jeremy, afford to be here?" Kenzie suddenly wondered.

"Sugar mama," Maxie said, before heading off to see her personal masseuse. "Rich girlfriend. Much older."

That gave Kenzie food for thought during the most luxurious massage she'd ever experienced: warm sheets, heated neck-roll, aromatherapy candles, calming new-age music, and the expert fingers of Thierry working on every muscle in her back, shoulders, arms, legs, and feet. Combined with the effect of the vodka, Kenzie was soon too blissed out to think about anything at all.

CHAPTER TEN

Horsing Around

The next day, Kenzie awoke at the crack of dawn. Her dream had come back, only this time with a "guest star"—a little girl, maybe three years old, was riding along with the woman on horseback. Like always, Kenzie had been floating peacefully, her cloud scudding lazily across the sky when she saw them. She had to descend far enough to see who the curly-topped tyke was. Only as usual, she wasn't fast enough. The woman on the horse was just out of reach. Kenzie could not catch up.

Her heart still hammering from the exertion, Kenzie pushed herself up on her elbows, shook herself fully awake. Was she going to be plagued by this dream every day for the next month? That would suck.

Maybe she should revisit the spa today. Yesterday's services, which had included a mani-pedi, shampoo, and styling, had kneaded away the hard knots of angst brought on by her first group therapy meeting. After being pampered and primped, she'd come back to her room, and immediately taken a nap on the zillion-thread-count bedding.

Kenzie had been pampered before, but she'd never spent this much time not working, not striving, not having to be someplace, please someone else, or put on an act? Maybe, as

Chelsea had said, she could try to think of Serenity Lake as the all-perks-included luxe vacation she'd never had?

Not that she'd want to spend any more time here than necessary. But as rehabs go, she figured, soaping herself in the shower with the organic shea butter cleanser, she felt lucky to have landed at Serenity Lake.

Unlike other facilities she'd read about, where patients, even celebrities, had to clean their own rooms, even scrub toilets and tubs (imagine!), Serenity Lake was a virtual Perks R Us, offering daily maid service, fresh linens and towels, gourmet meals, breakfast in bed if you wanted it. Retail therapy was available through an upscale gift shop.

And as long as Kenzie had Maxie—and the booze, pills, and power powder the girl seemed to have an endless supply of—rehab might be doable after all.

There were other options. She'd gotten daily notes urging her to participate in recovery-based activities. As Maxie had said, no one was forcing her, since celebrities were treated gingerly, but for Kenzie, if nothing else, being active would make the time pass even more quickly.

After breakfast she headed to the main activities office, where she was greeted effusively, and promptly assigned a head-spinning series of counselors, advisors, and therapists, each with a specific job to play in Kenzie's recovery—a joke, since she had nothing to recover from.

Aside from Dr. Wanderman and Emily, her personal nutritionist, she could soon be the proud, if temporary, owner of a personal recreational therapist; a spiritual care advisor, and a substance abuse counselor. After two weeks, if she wanted to go to AA meetings or any Serenity-sponsored field trip, she'd get her own off-campus chaperone.

Too much to contemplate. Kenzie considered doing a U-ie, heading back, and finding Maxie instead. If her friend was free (Maxie was obliged to take part in at least a minimum of activities), maybe they could hang out, pop some feel-good pills.

Then, Kenzie met her recreational therapist. Mike-with-the-mesmerizing-smile, she named him on the spot. An outdoorsy guy who rocked his scruff, he sported a real, from-the-sun tan, the first one Kenzie'd seen since being in L.A. Mike's handshake was firm and warm, which to Kenzie signaled strength and sincerity.

She stayed.

"We ask our guests to do at least one hour of physical activity every day," Mike explained as he walked Kenzie around the grounds, pointing out her choices.

Apparently, being active releases endorphins or endo-morphins or mighty morphins—Kenzie didn't catch it exactly. Just that they were in your body and had to be released, back into the wild or something. It was about creating a natural feeling of well-being. Without drugs, they meant.

Kind of the way she used to feel, before coming to Hollywood.

Mike took Kenzie to Serenity Lake's state-of-the-art fitness center, where she could choose a personal trainer to work out with. Kenzie crinkled her nose. She'd always found those machines scary and couldn't stand the music they always blared.

She nixed swimming. Though the pool was worthy, she had no cute bikinis here. Ditto, tennis.

The predawn meditative hikes were . . . well, predawn.

Another choice Mike mentioned was the climbing wall. "So you can face your fears," he explained.

Unless that wall's got a full-length mirror, Kenzie thought not.

Nothing interested her. Then Mike mentioned one last possibility: equine therapy.

Kenzie had never been up close and personal with a horse, let alone ridden one, but *The Horse Whisperer* was a great movie, and who doesn't like ponies? When Mike told her a new beginning class was starting later that afternoon, it sealed the deal. Kenzie signed up, even found herself looking forward to it.

Hours later, she realized she might have looked *into* it a little more. Mike-with-the-mesmerizing-smile hadn't mentioned the half-mile trek just to get to Serenity stables, located on the other side of the lake. In a posh place like this, had it been wrong for Kenzie to assume they'd bring the ponies to her?

When she finally found the stables, another thought hit her. She probably should have passed on the Maxie-provided marijuana at lunch earlier.

She'd spaced on how silly she gets when stoned.

Pony time began with a lecture. An older woman named Sue started by explaining the purpose of EAT, which stands for Equine-Assisted Therapy. Kenzie, feeling giddy, blurted that it was a poor choice of acronym for a rehab facility where half the patients are terrified to eat.

Several people gave her strange looks. Sue continued, "EAT is a metaphoric experience to promote emotional growth."

"Whose? Mine or the horse's?" Kenzie joked on. No one laughed.

"You'll learn about yourself, learn to recognize your dysfunctional patterns of behavior, and see what a healthy relationship—metaphorically speaking—looks like," Sue told the group.

"A relationship with a horse? What would my boyfriend say?" Kenzie quipped, woefully aware that she didn't have one right now.

"Horses are nonjudgmental and have no expectations or motives," Sue was saying, "so you don't have to fear rejection. The horse assists in making you aware of your real emotional state. It responds in reaction to your behavior."

There was more psychobabble, but what Kenzie gleaned was fairly simple. They'd each be assigned a personal pony to "join up with," and learn to take care of. Saddle it, bridle it, groom it, clean its hooves, feed it, and eventually, if guests wanted, ride it.

So far, so doable, Kenzie believed, until she heard the last part: They would be expected to clean up after it. Instantly, Kenzie was over EAT. 'Cause the idea of her—the "next big thing"—a shovel and pony poop was not happening.

She turned to leave when the assistants brought the horses out, and Kenzie was assigned hers. Instantly, she was smitten. This perfect creature was Brad Pitt.

Probably not his real name, but that's what Kenzie *had* to call him. He was gorgeous, a sleek, golden palomino with a white forelock, silky mane, and soulful eyes. If Kenzie were Angelina, she'd adopt him.

She followed Sue and Brad Pitt to a private small corral.

She was about to hoist herself up on the top wooden slat, because that's what they do in Westerns, but Sue closed the corral gate, and instructed Kenzie to stand in the center alongside her.

Brad Pitt was locked out of the corral. He looked so forlorn, just standing there. His expression (who knew horses could have expressions?) reminded Kenzie of Seth last year when her brother had been shut out of the school basketball team. So hurt.

"I'm pretty sure he wants to come inside the corral," Kenzie said. "Can you let him in?"

"That's very intuitive," Sue responded with a big smile. "It shows you're a compassionate person. We shut him out because his natural instinct is to be part of a herd or crowd. In this instance, we're the crowd."

"So we're deliberately icing him?" she asked, puzzled. "For no reason?"

"Our purpose is show him that *we're* in charge and that we'll take care of him."

"Why can't I just give him a carrot?" Kenzie wanted to know.

"You can, but first, you want him to choose to bond with you."

"I have to play hard to get?" she deduced. "It's like that with horses, too, huh?"

Sue furrowed her brow, uncomprehending.

"Okay, Kenzie, watch carefully. Tomorrow, this is what you'll be doing."

From inside the ring, Sue began waving her arms in front

of Brad, as if she were angry with him, stomping around, like she was chasing him away.

It looked really silly, but Kenzie had the feeling Brad had been down this road before. He got the memo. He began trotting outside the corral. Sue let him go around in circles, before getting up in his face again, repeating her faux-angry motions again. Brad did a U-ie, trotting counterclockwise outside the ring.

Oh, yeah. He's so done this with other girls before.

"Did you see that?" Sue asked after Brad had done several circles.

"See what?" Kenzie was clueless.

"Your horse just gave an important signal. He moved his jaw side to side in a chewing motion and flicked his ears," she pointed out.

Really? That was a signal? Not twitching at a fly?

"Watch carefully for what he does next," she instructed.

Brad wasn't doing anything. He just stood there staring. He was so expressive, Kenzie's heart went out to him. "Can we let him in now? Please."

Sue nodded happily. "You're going to get so much out of equine therapy, Kenzie. I'm so thrilled you choose it."

Kenzie started toward the gate, but Sue intervened. "As soon as we open the gate to let him in, we're going to turn our backs on him and walk to the center of the ring. Then we're going to stand there and lower our heads."

"We finally let him in, only to turn away from him?" Kenzie was confused. "That's cold."

"Be patient," Sue said as she opened the gate, took

Kenzie's hand, and led her pupil to the center of the ring. Kenzie followed Sue's lead, turned away, bowed her head. She felt beyond ridiculous, until she heard the clip-clop of hooves approaching.

"Can I look up now?" she whispered to Sue.

"Not yet. Let him come to you."

"He's right behind us," she whispered. "I can feel his hot breath. When do I get to turn around?"

"You'll know," she said softly.

True. Kenzie did know. All at once, the combination of grass, leather, and horse scent overwhelmed her. She felt Brad Pitt's snout in her hair as if he wanted a whiff of her shampoo.

"He's snuffling your hair," Sue said quietly.

Kenzie tried to stand completely still, not wanting the horse to turn away. He responded by coming even closer, and actually resting his head on Kenzie's shoulder.

He let out a soft neighing sound out.

Kenzie exhaled. And melted. Something about this moment felt so sweet, so right. Kenzie wasn't one to overthink, but if this was recovery therapy? Count her on the road.

"Now that was really interesting," Sue mused. "I gave him the directions, but he came straight to you. He wanted to join up with you."

"Most guys do," Kenzie quipped, turning to wink at Brad Pitt.

Most, but tragically, not all, she thought afterward. She was nuzzling Brad Pitt's neck, whispering that she'd be back tomorrow, when, out of the corner of her eye, she saw someone trotting toward the stable. Someone on horseback, that is.

Jeremy.

Kenzie checked him out.

Wishing she hadn't. Jeremy had made his contempt for Kenzie clear. She felt the same way toward him. Too bad he looked so hot astride a horse or, she admitted, hunched by the lake or tipping his chair backward during group therapy.

She couldn't help herself. She dawdled by the stables, watching him dismount, unbridle his horse, unbuckle the saddle, and hang it on the wall hook. A vision of them riding horseback together drifted by—she blinked, sending it packing.

When Jeremy saw her, he rolled his eyes, shook his head.

What the . . . ! Was that some comment on her taking equine therapy? Kenzie marched up, got right in his face, ready to confront him. Only . . . what Maxie had said about him having it really tough, the whole drug-dependency thing came back to her. She lost her nerve. All that she came up with was, "Are you taking equine therapy too, or horseback riding?"

"Both. Began with EAT, now I'm riding." Jeremy started off toward the villas. He did not make eye contact.

"Ever ridden before?" she asked.

"Oh, sure. Played pony polo at the club with my old man every Saturday," he said caustically.

"Umm, do-over?" she asked in her most adorable manner. "I should think before I speak."

"Good idea," he said, heading down the path leading back to main campus.

"Still, you look pretty comfortable on horseback," she said, hoping a compliment would undo her careless comment. "How long after joining up did you start to ride?"

"Don't remember," he mumbled, clearly uninterested in conversation.

It seemed important to forge ahead, anyway. If Jeremy had been mocking her, well . . . time to straighten him out, Kenzie decided.

"I've never been this close to a horse before," she informed him. "But I chose equine therapy because it sounded interesting."

Jeremy didn't comment.

"Technically, I don't have to take part in any of the activities," Kenzie confided. "I'll probably skip the rest."

"You're not doing yourself any favors," Jeremy said, not bothering with eye contact. "You don't think you need to be here, but the reality is, you are. Why not make the most of it?"

"That's exactly what I'm doing."

"I *mean*," he said deliberately, "why not take it seriously?"

"I am—" Kenzie started to protest, but even to her own ears, it sounded like the fib it was. She'd come to the stables slightly stoned, made jokes during the lecture, nearly bolted when they mentioned the poop. But once she met Brad Pitt, she sobered up. Seriously.

"You never know, you might need to learn to ride

for a film role." Jeremy was taking longer strides.

"That's what stunt doubles are for," Kenzie explained, quickening her pace to catch up.

"I know you think you're above the rest of us," he snapped, "but even you, Kenzie Cross, superstar, can benefit from being here."

"Have *you* benefited by being here? Are you off drugs for good?" she challenged him, hiding an unexpected hurt.

Jeremy had sped up. That last line was delivered to his back. Which is why they ended up crashing into each other when he did an abrupt U-turn.

"At this moment," Jeremy said, backing away from Kenzie, "I think it's safe to say I'm doing a lot fewer drugs than you are."

He stared at her fiercely, forcing Kenzie to cast her eyes downward and mumble, "I don't know what you're talking about."

"Cut the bull," he said. "I know you're using. I know you're high right now."

"Whaaaat? No way." She turned away from him.

He grasped her chin, forced her to look into his eyes. They were so pale, Kenzie saw, almost translucent. *Windows to his soul,* she thought.

"I can see it," he said. "You're stoned."

Inexplicably—and for no reason she could imagine—she blurted the stupidest thing that ever came out of her mouth. "The horse didn't!"

Jeremy's jaw dropped. So did his hand, no longer touching her face.

"I mean," she sputtered, "horses are supposed to be intuitive and metaphorical. Well, how come Brad Pitt chose to join up with me? He should've intuited that I was high. If I was high. Which I wasn't. And so he didn't."

Jeremy shook his head in disbelief. Then he stalked away.

CHAPTER ELEVEN

Om, Om on the Range

Jeremy's sarcastic outburst—". . . *even you, Kenzie Cross, superstar, can benefit from being here"* rankled. Kenzie wished she had a scriptwriter to give her a snappy comeback, a line of dialog to put Jeremy in his place. On her own, she was not that clever. On her own, she couldn't put a cohesive sentence together, or so it had seemed.

Why should she even care what he thought? Jeremy was just some random rehab guy. Besides, she'd never had to justify herself, or work to get a guy to like her. Most people liked her. So what if one or two, like Jeremy, or Doug from group therapy, didn't? What was she, some stereotypical, self-absorbed, narcissistic actress who *needed* to be loved by *everyone*? If that were true, when exactly had she turned into a cliché?

If she were to discontinue equine therapy, Kenzie decided as she paced her room, if she were to choose another activity, it would not be because of Jeremy Haven.

She thought of yoga. Yoga *had* been on her to-do list ever since she'd gotten to Hollywood and found out everyone in showbiz does some form of it. No matter what the latest fitness craze is, eventually, they all come back *om*.

So there. Or something. Too much thinking, too much introspection made Kenzie's head hurt.

So when Maxie came along bearing gifts, Kenzie was grateful and more than a little delighted for the distraction. This time the bounty included a guaranteed stress-antidote in the form of a little oblong, coral-colored pill: Xanax.

Kenzie took two—and resolved to call her spiritual advisor in the morning.

She didn't make good on that resolution, at least not right away. The next day Kenzie returned to equine therapy instead, and then attended another group therapy session.

Maxie didn't even have to drag her. She wanted to go. To go sober even, prove to Jeremy that she was taking rehab seriously. Earn respect.

In the end, all it proved was a stupid mistake. All she got was beat up on.

"You admit to daily partying," Dr. Wanderman pointed out when Kenzie, under scrutiny of the group, tried to explain why she didn't need to be in rehab.

"Maybe it would help if you explained instead why you need to drink, to take painkillers?" Dr. Wanderman was so patient.

Exasperated, Kenzie tried to brush off the question.

"The need? It's just part of my job." She went on to say that in showbiz, it's essential to always look and feel at the top of your game—even if you have a hangover or some drama or you're just plain pooped.

"OMG! I totally understand," blurted Jenny. "You're doing it for your career. Me too! I'm a model, and if I'm going to get work, I cannot gain weight."

"But if you continue to lose weight, you'll starve. And last time I looked, dead people don't get too much work," Maxie said gently. "There's got to be a balance between overeating and starving yourself. You'll find it here. We'll help."

At that moment, Kenzie saw the family resemblance between Maxie and Lev. At heart, both were truly compassionate people.

"Jenny hates herself," Hannah exclaimed. "That's why she cuts herself."

Jenny teared up, and Maxie leaned over and draped a reassuring arm around the bony girl. "I don't think she hates herself. I think it's just the stupid pressure society puts on women to be skinny—especially models or entertainers in the public eye."

"So don't be a model," Doug declared as if that solved the problem. "Do something else."

Jenny was full-out sobbing. "I can't do anything else. I don't know how."

Unfortunately, the Jenny sidebar did not sidetrack Dr. Wanderman, who insisted that Kenzie continue.

Grudgingly, she told them that the people in charge of her career, Team Kenzie, sometimes need to score her uppers, which help her focus and do her job. At times, she got too wired or anxious. Valium, Xanax, or Vicodin were provided to take the edge off. It's the way it works in Hollywood. It's normal.

Judging by the skeptical looks of everyone but Maxie, no one shared her nonchalant view. She began to feel defensive and didn't like it one bit.

"At night, of course I go out. You have to keep your face out there. But mainly, I'm a social person. I've always had lots of friends. Even back home, we drank, we partied. It's fun. Being on TV hasn't changed me. That's who I am."

"Being on TV gives you access to an unlimited supply of alcohol and drugs. That's the difference," Dr. Wanderman pointed out.

Color me lucky, is what Kenzie was tempted to say.

"On some level," the shrinkess continued, "you know that taking advantage of it is dangerous and self-destructive."

On some level, Kenzie wanted to shout, *you* have no idea what it takes to be a star in this town.

Feeling misunderstood and under attack, Kenzie met with her spiritual care advisor the next afternoon. The woman was exactly as Kenzie had pictured: lithe, soft-spoken, dressed in flowy white top and loose pants. Her name was Farrah. She wore no makeup, was a natural beauty, exuding a peaceful, loving vibe. Just being around her gave Kenzie an unexpected sense of calm.

That was helpful, because the session turned out to be very different than she'd imagined. Kenzie assumed she'd spend the hour sitting pretzel-like, and contorting her body into a bunch of strange positions, like a game of spiritual Twister. All the while listening to woo-woo music and chanting *"om."*

Already, she'd planned her patter upon re-entering Hollywood. Lots of actresses claimed to have achieved their rockin' bods from yoga, but Kenzie knew otherwise: Botox, implants, face lifts, tummy tucks had likely played a part. *She* would not only rock some really cute yoga outfits, but would sound authentic, dropping buzz words like "downward dog" or "cobra."

Farrah ushered a sweatsuited Kenzie into Lotus Hall. There was nothing slick, state-of-the-art, or even posh about the space. Lotus Hall looked like it had wandered in from a nearby ashram and settled on Serenity Lake property. It was a stark space, low-carpeted, with an A-frame ceiling—completely empty except for an altar against the front wall, holding candles and incense and framed pictures of yogis who reminded Kenzie of Dumbledore. Yet, there was something warm and safe about this bare-bones space.

Farrah offered her a yoga mat, along with a beat-up throw pillow. The spiritual advisor dimmed the lights and lit two candles and an incense stick. Again, Kenzie had the strangest sensation of calm, like being held inside a protective, peaceful bubble. Weird. Especially since she was completely sober.

Farrah's voice had something to do with it. It was lilting, serene, tranquil, almost hypnotic. "Yoga teaches you many things. The form we'll be practicing is called 'integral.' We focus on the spiritual aspect. We believe in sending peaceful, healing, loving thoughts out in the world. As part of your recovery therapy, it will help you to be in touch with your body, release your tensions, be aware of your breathing, and your chakras. You will learn the peace of total relaxation, and find your true self."

Kenzie had not given much thought to the spiritual aspect. All her life, she'd been pretty sure she knew her true self.

Maybe it was Farrah herself or the understanding that she wouldn't be competing with anyone, but Kenzie took to yoga immediately. This wasn't a class dotted with faux-spiritual showbiz types, no one was showing off, there was no one to show off to. It was just her, free to be.

As Farrah guided her through the warm-up exercises, Kenzie felt a sensation not just of well-being, but of doing the right thing, being in the right head space. Somehow.

She decided not to overthink it.

Even when Farrah taught her the first asana, called the sun salutation, and Kenzie had trouble with the pose, just trying felt good. Farrah patiently helped her, explaining it didn't matter how long it took her to catch on. Whatever pace Kenzie was at was the right pace for herself.

Then, she learned deep relaxation. Farrah taught her the corpse position—lying on her back, arms extended by her side, palms up.

Eyes closed, Kenzie followed Farrah's directions, which involved the simple tensing up, then complete relaxing, of all the body parts, one by one. Before Kenzie knew it, she'd fallen into a kind of trancelike state. Awake enough to hear her teacher, but mentally, definitely elsewhere. Without any chemical assistance. Interesting.

It was during her very first time practicing deep relaxation that out of nowhere, a picture formed. A blond woman was hoisting baby Kenzie in the air, cooing, "Twinkle, twinkle, little star." The picture, like a movie frame, lasted a moment only, then disappeared. Long enough, however, for an unbridled, unfiltered sense of pure joy and fulfillment to wash over her.

Tears followed. Big, gloppy, and totally unexpected. Embarrassed, Kenzie tried to wipe them away, but her spiritual advisor was not surprised, was pleased, even. "When the body is truly in deep relaxation," she explained to Kenzie, "many people find long-buried memories come awake. Some people smile, some laugh, some cry, some are scared.

"You don't have to tell me what you saw, Kenzie. But it seems like this holds some deeper meaning for you. You should think about it."

CHAPTER TWELVE

Maxie's Midnight Confession

That first yoga session left Kenzie in a hazy daze. She headed back toward her room in Villa Primrose, unsure what she'd gotten out of it, but decidedly not interested in pondering the images and feelings the deep relaxation exercise had brought up.

There were other ways to relax deeply. One of them was sitting on the steps of her villa, wearing a wicked smile, a tattered pink T-shirt, and new shocking pink streaks in her black hair.

"What's up, Pinkberry smoothie?" Kenzie smiled broadly at Maxie.

"I have a verrrry special treat for you," she said mischievously.

"Hmmm . . . animal, vegetable, or mineral?" Kenzie kidded.

"Chemical. But you'll have to wait to receive it."

Waiting was not so much a Kenzie Cross specialty. "How long?"

"Not very," said Maxie, looking like a kid with a match who could barely wait to set off the fireworks.

• • •

After an insanely fabulous dinner featuring fresh baked dinner rolls, barbecued chicken, garlic mashed potatoes, and organic salad, Maxie motioned for Kenzie to follow her outside.

"Are we breaking out?" Kenzie asked, half-joking.

"Not today," she said, not joking at all.

They headed around the back of the villas to the lap pool. It was after hours, no one was around.

"Skinny-dipping?" Kenzie guessed.

"Better," Maxie said, pointing to the cabanas.

The cabanas were a revelation—more luxe than any Kenzie had seen previously. Inside were two large cushioned lounge chairs, a snack table, a mini fridge stocked with iced tea and bottled water, a small fan, and a cabinet with sunscreen, flip-flops, and pool towels.

Maxie drew the woven canvas curtains together, fastening them closed with canvas ties. Then, she fished around behind the mini fridge.

Out came what resembled an ornate candlestick, with a bulbous glass base and two small hoses attached: a hookah!

Flashback! Kenzie had not smoked out of a hookah since sophomore year in high school. Her memories were all kickback, good times.

The beauty of a hookah, as Kenzie recalled, is that it can be used to smoke anything, like tobacco and flavored shisha, which is completely legal. It can also be used for not-so-legal substances.

"I'm not even going to ask you how you managed to sneak this in, but what about the spy-cams?" Kenzie said, watching Maxie expertly assemble the hookah.

"That, my friend, is the beauty and the dirty little secret of the cabanas. No cameras." Her eyes glittered.

"Why not?"

"Who cares?" Maxie said with a shrug, lighting the charcoal. When the embers were glowing, she put the hose to her mouth, and took a savory hit. She closed her eyes, and sighed, "Aaahhh. So good."

Kenzie didn't wait to be invited. She picked up the second hose. It didn't take long for the drug to kick in and create a lovely, slightly off-center, hazy-dazey head space.

"The cabanas are where everyone goes to hook up," Maxie reminded Kenzie.

"Hookahs? Everyone hides them here?"

Maxie giggled. "Not hooo-kahs. Hookups. As in sex."

Kenzie raised my eyebrows. "Really? And you know this how?"

"Anyone who's done multiple stints at Serenity Lake knows it. Most have firsthand knowledge."

"Anyone I know?" *Please don't say Jeremy.* Kenzie swatted that unbidden thought away.

"People you might not expect. Like our group therapy buddy, Doug, has had a few encounters of the physical kind here," she said.

"Ewww! Batwing Brows?" Kenzie choked on the smoke, forgetting how hard it is to talk and inhale at the same time.

Maxie cracked up. "Batwing Brows? You oughta try calling him that to his face—it'll only set his therapy back ten years."

"Seriously," Kenzie said, laughing, "who'd want to hook up with him?"

"Doug's got his issues, but he is a guy and he's straight. And if you, Miss Thing, could manage to peel your baby blues off Jeremy Haven for two seconds, you'd realize that the pickings are pretty slim around here," Maxie teased her.

"How many times do I have to tell you I'm not into him?" Kenzie protested.

"Until it's true," Maxie shot back. "Anyway, rehab hookups are like that famous song, 'If you can't be with the one you love, love the one you're with,'" she trilled.

In the two group sessions Kenzie had been to, both times Doug sat next to Hannah. The picture of tiny self-loathing Hannah and her casts doing it with big ol' fragile-ego Batwing Brows set off a giggle fit. When Kenzie told Maxie what was so funny, the laughter doubled.

Kenzie just couldn't help herself, she started to sing and pantomime, "If you can't be with the one you love, love with the one you're stuck with!" Tears of weed-fueled laughter streamed down her face.

"Wait! I have a better one," Maxie squealed. "If you can't hook up with the one you want, hookah with the one you can!"

They kept one-upping each other, all the while taking tandem tokes, and breaking out into gales of laughter. They were their own best audience.

Though the tent curtains were closed, a breeze blew in from outside. Related or not, Kenzie suddenly experienced a perfect moment of coherence, one thin sliver of lucidity pierced the happy haze of a brain on bong.

Maxie was singing. Kenzie heard her—really heard her—for the first time.

Damn! Maxie was good. Like Christina Aguilera good, Mariah Carey, Whitney Houston good.

"You've got pipes!" Kenzie blurted.

"Just the one," Maxie giggled, indicating the hookah.

"You know what I mean," Kenzie persisted. "You can sing. I am not hallucinating, you've got an amazing voice. And range. You're . . . you're . . . pitchy! You'd kill on *American Idol*."

"Do they allow stoners on that show?" she teased.

"I'm serious! You have to try out. My agents can hook you up." Kenzie felt proud that she could do a solid for Maxie.

Maxie put the bong down, let her head loll back on the lounger, and closed her eyes.

Maxie was slim, small-boned, and underneath the choppy black-and-pink hair, gobs of eyeliner, multi-piercings, and tats, probably very pretty. Right now, she looked less like a goth rebel than a little girl playing dress up. Vulnerable. Fragile, Kenzie concluded. Which led to the question she didn't know she was going to ask. "Why did you call yourself a 'fragile little failure' that day after group therapy?"

Maxie squinted and cast a sideways glance at Kenzie. "You still on the *American Idol* tip?"

She knew differently.

Clearly Maxie hadn't planned on baring her soul. It was just Kenzie didn't want to let her off the hook. She didn't even know why it was important to figure Maxie out. Just that it was.

Maxie tried to wiggle out of talking. She pretended to be asleep. She fronted that she'd just been messing around, made it up.

Kenzie wasn't buying it. She prodded.

"Why's it so important to you?" Maxie whined. "My saga, as you call it, is beyond boring."

Kenzie coaxed.

"It's worse than boring. It's a complete cliché."

Kenzie badgered.

Eventually, after several more deeply inhaled tokes, Maxie gave it up, unrolled the story like a red carpet on Oscar night. Kenzie listened attentively.

"My parents, Cecilia and Angelo Romano, are stars of the Los Angeles Opera—you probably know that. They were both musical prodigies and trained for years to perform professionally. They've always been totally passionate about their art."

Maxie paused, then took another toke. "It was no big secret that they assumed—hoped—for a child who'd inherit their gift."

"Lev didn't?" Kenzie guessed.

"Have you heard him sing? He sounds like the shrieking spawn of K-Fed and Bjork," she cracked.

"Point taken," Kenzie agreed.

"They tried for more kids, but alas, the well was dry after Lev. At the time, adoption—especially of an Asian girl—was all the rage in their social and political circles. I was in an orphanage in China, the soloist in choir."

Kenzie shot Maxie a suspicious look. "Tell me this isn't going where I think it is. They adopted you because it was the 'in' thing to do *and* so they could make you into an opera singer?" That was so ridiculous, Kenzie snort-giggled as she said it.

Maxie? Not giggling. "They weren't searching for a musical prodigy. But when they found me . . . and it just so happened I was Lev's exact age and we shared the same birthday, how could they not think it was fate, God's plan all along?"

Kenzie conceded it was possible. But probable? Too strange.

"I felt like the chosen child, the special, golden girl," Maxie said. As she ingested more of the drug, more of her story rolled out. "I'd been adopted at six years old, by a wealthy, loving American family, and I had an instant twin. I was in heaven. Naturally, I went along with the program. I was always taking lessons, in voice, diction, and classical music. I sang my little heart out, day in and day out. I'd have done anything for them."

"You loved them," Kenzie said.

"I wanted to be the girl they wanted me to be. The two of them, they kept the dream alive, even though after a while, my teachers were in agreement: Maxie is a very talented girl, but no matter how hard she works, she's never going to perform professionally," Maxie croaked. She stopped abruptly to wipe away a tear.

Kenzie felt for her. "I'm guessing your parents didn't believe it."

"They hired new teachers. I tried harder. Eventually, I got my first role. I was going to play Fredrika in the L.A. Opera's *A Little Night Music.*

"It was this major big deal. At home, there was lots of celebrating, more intense practicing, leaving school early for rehearsals, more tutoring. I'd made them so proud, I couldn't have been happier."

"What happened?" Kenzie asked cautiously.

"Opening night," Maxie said, taking another drag from the pipe, "that's what happened."

"You weren't that great?"

"I wasn't anything. I looked out into the audience—and froze. My throat closed. I couldn't make a sound. I ran offstage. It was the most humiliating moment of my life. And theirs."

Kenzie would never forget the expression on Maxie's face: She looked like a crumpled, used tissue. "But you were a kid!" Kenzie cried. "And they were your parents. They wouldn't hold that against you.'

"They didn't—not to my face. But I knew. I was a certified disappointment. I was ten by that time. If I was destined to follow in their footsteps, it'd have happened by then. It began to be clearer and clearer to me—" Maxie choked, unable to get the rest out.

Kenzie wished she hadn't.

"I knew then they were sorry they ever adopted me," Maxie sobbed quietly into her torn T-shirt.

Kenzie leaned over and draped her arm around her small-boned friend. "They never said that, no one would be that cruel."

"They didn't have to. It was obvious."

"Listen to yourself," Kenzie said. "This is crazy. You're not super-opera-girl, ergo, you're unworthy? What does Lev say?"

Maxie wiped her face on her sleeves, and sniffed, "Oh, my parents are equal opportunity disappointment-finders. We're twin failures."

Later, before drifting off to sleep, Kenzie thought about her dad. No matter what she accomplished—or tried and failed at—his love for her was unconditional. He was always proud of her.

And somewhere, her mom was too.

CHAPTER THIRTEEN

Maxie had assured her they would not be caught for their latest infraction. Still, Kenzie was shocked at not being busted for their evening of hookah hilarity. That cabana had to have reeked of weed. She could only assume that without spy-cams, the Serenity Lake staff couldn't pin it on anybody.

After several days had passed, and no one came a-scolding, Kenzie had to once again give it up for Maxie Romano. The girl knew her way around rehab. Maxie also offered to sneak messages out for Kenzie, who was a couple days shy of the two-week mark, still barred from outside communication.

Kenzie was finding it harder and harder to maintain the level of righteous resentment, disappointment, and feelings of betrayal toward Chelsea, Gabe, and Lev. Not because she suddenly saw the light or the wisdom of their arguments for rehab. Maybe yoga had mellowed her, maybe Brad Pitt had a forgiving effect on her.

During Maxie's allowed hour online, she contacted Kenzie's peeps, even printed out the responses.

Each of them assured Kenzie they totally missed her. But reading about all the fun they were having "on the outside," Kenzie wondered. They were out every night, hitting the clubs, the bottles, the boys (Chelsea and Gabe) and girls (Lev). There was a new guy in Gabe's life, a keeper, he hoped, as well as several new clubs he might be promoting. Chelsea was trying a new diet and, fingers crossed, results were excellent. Chelsea also wrote about a rumor that the famous actress Sherry Sweeney was at Serenity Lake.

Kenzie was about to debunk the rumor, when she flashed on the familiar-looking detox lady in the hallway with the haunted eyes.

Instantly, Kenzie put it together.

Sherry Sweeney had been a huge movie star. A decade ago, when she was around Kenzie's age, she'd starred in a string of successful teen and chick movies. There had been whispers of substance abuse, but back then, when there weren't paparazzi around every corner to record them, they were never proven. Sherry simply faded from the radar. Everyone forgot her.

The more Kenzie thought about it, the more convinced she became that detox-lady wasn't Sherry. That sorrowful woman looked ancient, forty even.

Maybe it was the Sherry Sweeney saga or the simple pleasure of remembering what words on a page looked like or nighttime boredom (she and Maxie were laying low for a couple more nights, just in case); something spurred Kenzie to look for something to read. She wasn't allowed access to magazines and wasn't into books.

She rooted around in her duffel for the only thing at hand—the screenplay for *The Chrome Hearts Club*. At least, she thought, thumbing through it, it was short, only 120 pages. At worst, it'd put her to sleep.

It blew her mind. Kenzie had started to read just before bedtime and could not put the thing down. After the first five pages, she recognized the story as completely superior to any *Spywitness Girls* script.

The Chrome Hearts Club was about the lives of a band of troubled teens, kids on the fringes of society, without family, who fall through the cracks, usually end up dead or behind bars. These ragtag juvies form their own family, trying to pull each other up, with mixed results.

It was far, far from Kenzie's life, but as written, it sure felt like somebody's gritty life experience. It read real, so opposite the superficial cartoony *Spywitness Girls*. It was, Kenzie mused, more like *The Outsiders*, one of Kenzie's all-time favorites. That book took place in the Oklahoma of the 1960s. *The Chrome Hearts Club* was now, juxtaposing the dark alleyways of downtown Los Angeles against the opulence of Beverly Hills.

Her character, Sarah, was complex, a foster-care runaway who ended up a street urchin. It was her idea to bring the others together; she was the heart and soul of the club.

As she pondered the inner life of her character, Kenzie's mind raced. She could think of several different ways to play the role. By the time she got to the end, she'd determined that her first official e-mail was going to Daniel Lightstorm, the director.

First, she'd get on her Internet knees and apologize. The young director really had taken a huge risk casting her.

This was a star-making role, and it was going to a girl

who'd had but one TV part, and then went on TV interviews, trivializing the film. The stupid comment she'd made to that TV host, inviting him to "join" the club, came back to bite her. She was to have promoted the film, but all she'd done was prove herself to be a ditz. Kenzie was ashamed, but determined to redeem herself.

If nothing else, the stint in rehab gave her a second chance at the movie. She was now truly grateful for that.

Kenzie had to hope that the next two and half weeks, the time she had left to serve, would pass quickly and quietly, that nothing would happen to jeopardize the deal.

So far, her friends had informed her, Milo's plan to keep her whereabouts a secret was working. Kenzie had not been outed in the tabloids as Rehab Girl. As she drifted off to sleep that night, she wondered what the odds of her rehab stint *staying* buried were.

Slim. And none.

That was her answer. It arrived on a tabloid platter, two days later.

She'd just come back to her villa after a yoga session, feeling very Zen, very centered, and very looking forward to diving back into the script. That's when Maxie had burst in, clutching an illegal BlackBerry, because, she explained breathlessly, "You need to hear this from me."

It had started, like any venal virus, online. Specifically, on CelebrityDish.com.

The Mystery of the Disappearing Kenzie! It's been twelve nights in a row, and Kenzie Cross has not come out to play. Where, oh where, has our little starlet gone? Professional club-kid Gabe Waxworth pleads ignorance. Slacker Lev Romano growls, "She's allowed to stay in if she wants to. Get off my back!" Kenzie's avowed "homegirl" Chelsea Piers says she thinks Kenzie went to visit her aunt. In Omaha. She thinks? That girl is attached at the hip to Kenzie. Pul-eeze. Do Ms. Piers, Mr. Waxworth, and Mr. Romano think we won't check?

Kenzie felt sick. Not so much about being exposed—she should have realized all those days without slippage had been miraculous—but *that* was the best her BFFs could come up with? Gabe, Lev, and Chelsea might as well have taken out a billboard on Sunset Strip. Or just hit default and told the reporter she was being treated for "dehydration and exhaustion." An aunt in Omaha?

Obvious translation: Kenzie's in rehab.

Q: Was it naive to hope that it'd take them a while to figure out *where* she was? Enough time so Milo could spin it as they'd plotted? That this was *pre*-hab; it's Kenzie being proactive, that going to rehab was precautionary?

A: Not just naive. Truly stupid.

Maxie, with at least a half dozen tabloids tucked under her arm, intercepted Kenzie on the way to breakfast the next morning. The newspapers were amazingly similar, Kenzie had been served up as the cover girl-du-jour. She glanced at them, horrified. She hadn't known so many bad pictures of her even existed. She looked fat. And drugged out, too.

"How'd you get all of these?" she asked Maxie, as the two settled themselves on a bench.

"I have a friend on staff here," Maxie finally admitted.

"A friend . . . on your payroll?" Kenzie hated herself for saying that.

"Don't bite the messenger," Maxie said. "Besides, it's not as if you haven't enjoyed the favors my friend has supplied all this week too."

"Sorry. I'm just freaked. Forgive?" Kenzie chastised herself for the "on your payroll" comment. Maxie had shown herself to be a true friend in a very short time. She'd confided in Kenzie and had her back.

"I'll go burn these," she now promised.

"Not before I see them." Kenzie sounded like a typical Hollywood narcissist-slash-masochist. The type she used to mock.

Unsurprisingly, the headlines were epically unoriginal.

Starlet in Rehab!

Kenzie Crosses (get it?) the Line!

Kenzie: Heir to the Lindsay Throne!

Exclusive! *Spywitness* to a Drug Problem!

The articles, which quoted numerous "sources" and "insiders"—none of whom were named—were as original as the headlines. All were variations of the same sad, sordid tale:

> *America's honeymoon with starlet on the rise Kenzie Cross is over. Looks like the erstwhile wholesome TV star has officially flamed out.*
>
> *Our inside source has partied with Kenzie and witnessed the underage star drinking copious*

*amounts of tequila and snorting cocaine, crushing
rumors that her rehab stint is nothing more than a
publicity stunt. But is she serious about cleaning up
her act? Or is this just another starlet in pseudo-
therapy, spending a month relaxing in an exclusive
resort, getting tanned, toned, and practicing her "I
see the error of my ways, forgive me," speech?*

*Kenzie's costars refused to go on record, but
dropped clues that suspicion of drug use has long
been an issue on set. When asked about her future
on the show, they admitted they'd heard rumors
that talks were going on about replacing her.*

Replace her? With one of them? Right. When Posh Spice
wins a Nobel Prize in science.

Kenzie's anger turned into righteous fury. The lies—and
exaggerations! She'd flamed out? People suspected her of
drug use on the *Spywitness* set? It made her sound like a
crackhead.

Kenzie's blood was boiling; bitter bile rose in her throat.

"You okay?" Maxie asked doubtfully.

"I will be," she said through gritted teeth.

Kenzie used to laugh these stories off. So what if this
cut closer to the truth than others had? She'd never cared
before. What had changed?

She took a deep, cleansing breath and tried not to
care now.

Didn't work.

Right in the middle of campus, under Maxie's uncomprehending eyes, she slipped off the bench, settled into

the lotus position on the grass, and tried to concentrate on releasing all that bad energy. She chanted, felt the reverberations throughout her body. She watched her breathing and waited to calm down.

Instead, she bolted up. Kenzie couldn't do yoga by herself. She was too new at it. Telling Max she'd see her later, Kenzie strode off toward the yoga center. Maybe she'd get lucky and Farrah, her instructor, would be available.

It was a plan.

Might've worked too, but Farrah had the day off and Kenzie didn't want to try a new instructor.

She tried a massage, but it didn't take her mind off the tabloids. She sulked through her pedicure, got impatient waiting for her manicure to dry.

During her facial, Maxie came bearing a printout of an *Us Weekly* online column. One nasty blog-hound bumped against the truth, Maxie informed her.

Quickly, Kenzie peeled the cucumbers off her eyes, and read:

Have allegations of drug and alcohol abuse about TV starlet Kenzie Cross jeopardized her starring role in Daniel Lightstorm's The Chrome Hearts Club? *Her representatives deny it, but I have it on good authority that the director ordered her to rehab—or she's off the picture.*

Chills ran down Kenzie's spine. She thought she might upchuck.

If no one came forward to deny that article, to stop it from spreading, Kenzie could be truly screwed. No one would believe the pre-hab bull; she'd be regarded as just another screwup with a drug problem, forced into rehab.

That night, she needed more pills to chill. Even Maxie warned her to ease up.

The next day, Kenzie made for equine-assisted therapy. It wasn't on her schedule, but hanging out with Brad Pitt, her own private stud, had a definite calming effect.

Once or twice, Kenzie had tried talking to him. She'd felt silly, but weirdly he seemed to understand.

Kenzie had just begun learning the first steps in grooming a horse, cleaning his saddle, bridle, and halter. When she got to the stables, she asked permission to try it by herself.

Her equine-assisted therapist, Sue, was cool with it. "Just holler if you need me. I'll be right outside."

Kenzie thanked her profusely. Concentrating on taking care of Brad's stuff would take her mind off the tabloids, and the scary fact that not one of Team Kenzie had responded to her frantic e-mails-via-Maxie. Not Alex, nor Rudy, nor the one who should have been all over it, Milo.

No news, in this case, was *not* good news.

Kenzie forced herself to focus on the task at hand. She removed the saddle from its hook on the wall, grabbed some saddle soap, a damp cloth, and a bucket of water. The more she thought about the hateful things written about her and the awful pictures they printed, the harder she worked. Brad Pitt stared at her in wonder, as she put some serious elbow grease into the task.

Kenzie chuckled. "Probably when you first joined up with me, you thought two gorgeous movie stars should stick together. You don't know my backstory. I wasn't always a pampered diva. I used to vacuum, do dishes, scrub the tub, and after school, pick up my baby brother from day care and babysit him."

Brad nickered softly.

She hadn't even realized she'd been talking out loud to the horse.

"I didn't mind doing any of it," Kenzie continued. "It felt good to help my dad out. None of my friends knew. They'd probably have called me Cinderella or something. I had an image to keep up. I was the popular girl on her way to Hollywood."

Brad let out a snort.

"Anyway, I think that's the reason my dad was lenient with me, let me go out at night, stay out late. He figured I deserved it. And he trusted me. Back then anyway. Now, he trusts the tabloids."

In response, Brad kicked the dirt under his hooves.

By the time Kenzie put some spit-shine on the saddle, she'd accepted at least this much: Unless another wayward starlet stole the spotlight, the story about getting dumped from the movie would spread like a Malibu wildfire. And then what? Would her career be left standing or turn into so much ash?

She left the stables, unaware that she'd soon have something bigger to worry about. There was another tabloid, out that very day. This one carried an even more personal exposé.

CHAPTER FOURTEEN

If It's Not One Thing, It's Your Mother

Kenzie had the Pudgy Prince of Paranoia to thank for picking up on the one tabloid Maxie had missed.

It happened at group therapy. She knew something was up the minute she crested the hill. The smirk on Doug's face was aimed squarely at her, as was a telltale tabloid he brandished. "Nice job keeping rehab under wraps," he sneered.

Had the karma gods spoken already? Maybe the night she'd mocked him doing hookah with Maxie was coming back at her? she thought guiltily.

"Why do you even care?" Kenzie bristled. "There are no pictures of you, hence, no paparazzi hiding under the palm trees."

"This article affects all of us in group," Doug retorted.

"How?" Maxie challenged.

"Because it exposes you for the fraud you are!" Doug shot back.

Kenzie was confused. She'd assumed Doug was referring to the story about Daniel threatening to fire her. The whole rehab-by-blackmail thing. She was starting to get the feeling, a very bad feeling, that today, Doug's slingshot was armed with a different kind of ammo. She willed herself to play it cool. "Are they saying I'm a fraud as an actress?"

"More like a fraud as a person," he spat. "You've been playing us, insisting you only drink and take drugs because it's part of your job. You have no issues, no addictions. Meanwhile, we sit here, baring our souls, trying to help each other through real-life crises, beat our addictions, it's like we're just performing for the starlet's amusement, like jesters around Queen Above-it-all."

"Did we really need the essay answer?" Kenzie groused, trying to keep herself from panicking.

"According to this article," Doug detailed, "your life hasn't been so perfect. It tells us the real reason for your substance-abuse issues. You're just self-medicating, like the rest of us."

Kenzie's stomach began to twist itself into a knot. She couldn't even guess what Doug was babbling about. She looked at Maxie for a clue, but her friend was as puzzled as she.

"Enough, Doug," Dr. Wanderman finally interrupted his rant. "Whatever it is you've got there is infuriating *you*. That's not healthy."

Doug nodded to the therapist, tried to keep his voice level. "Okay. But once I read this, I won't be the only one who's pissed at her."

Beads of sweat formed on Kenzie's forehead. She wished she could summon the *Spywitness Girls'* "Beauty Squad" to dab them away.

"May I see the newspaper?" Dr. Wanderman asked.

When he handed it over, Kenzie recognized the familiar logo of the *Enquirer*. She began to relax. Of all the tabloids, they were the least likely to print anything believable.

"What's it say?" Hannah asked.

"Let Dr. Wanderman read it first," said Jenny. "She'll tell us the real deal."

"Guys," Kenzie reminded everyone, "it's the *Enquirer*. It probably says I'm the daughter of a two-headed alien." She reached for a bottle of water.

"Actually, Kenzie," Dr. Wanderman said after scanning the article, "it says you're the daughter of a woman who abandoned your family."

A wave of cold fear, like nausea, washed over her. She heard her heart pounding.

"It's called 'Kenzie's Tragic Childhood Exposed!' Everyone's gotta hear this," Doug, vindicated, blurted.

"How would you feel about that?" the therapist asked. "Do you want to read it yourself, first?"

"What?" Had Kenzie heard correctly? Was Wanderman considering sharing it with the entire group? Panic rose like sour bile in her throat. Swallowing, she surveyed the group. Everyone, including Jeremy, was on the edge of their seats. Somehow, the actress in Kenzie kicked in. She wasn't giving them a show. "Knock yourself out," she said as breezily as possible, straightening her spine. "Whatever crap is in there is complete fabrication. But,"—she stared daggers at Wanderman—"if, in your medical opinion, you believe it's necessary take up everyone's time with a bunch of lies, that's your call. *Doctor.*

With one word, Kenzie had baited the doctor, questioning her professionalism.

"For the first time, I hear anger and vulnerability," Dr. Wanderman responded way too kindly. "And you're right, this is highly unorthodox and somewhat risky. But I'm wondering if by sharing this, it will turn out to be our first breakthrough—the one that allows us to really help you."

Kenzie gripped the bottom of her chair to control her shaking.

"I'll read it!" Doug was practically foaming at the mouth.

"It's better if I do," the shrinkess actually said. "Nothing salacious, one or two pertinent paragraphs."

"Hold on," Maxie finally spoke up. "This isn't right. We don't gang up on people in group."

Kenzie willed Jeremy to speak up for her too. He remained silent.

In a soft voice, Dr. Wanderman read the piece. It charted Kenzie's clubbing, drinking, drugging, in detail, ad nauseum. (Kenzie now got where *that* phrase came from.) Dr. Wanderman then got to the "meat" of the article.

"'No one in this close-knit Seattle suburb knows why Abigail Cross abandoned her husband, Alan; ten-year-old daughter, Mackenzie; and newborn son, Seth—only that she did. Abby Cross made no secret of it. Many neighbors and friends recall seeing her pack up the family sedan and drive off, waving good-bye to her bewildered daughter, who couldn't have known Mommy wasn't coming back.'

"'So what made Abby run? Postpartum depression, a grave illness? An affair with another man?'

"'According to her good friend, Pamela Piers, "Abby was an outgoing, joyful, free spirit, a good wife, and a loving mother. She especially adored Kenzie, she doted on the girl. That's why I felt so sorry for her when Abby left.""'"

Kenzie's cheeks burned, her throat closed. She wanted to yank the magazine away from this poseur, rip it to shreds. She had to sit on her hands to stop herself from sticking her fingers in my ears, shouting, "I can't hear you!" She concentrated on her breathing, on staying in character. Like a good actress. No one was going to see Kenzie Cross broken, humiliated.

Maxie reached over to take her hand, but Kenzie shook it off with a grateful smile, wishing she'd passed a couple of Xanax over.

"How do you react to this?" Dr. Wanderman looked at Kenzie with much empathy, the starlet wanted to smack her face.

"How do you think?" demanded Maxie. "That was unprofessional and uncalled for."

"It's okay, Max," Kenzie said calmly. "No one with a brain believes that melodrama. It's the *Enquirer*. It's all lies."

"It isn't *all* lies," Doug giddily put in. "They have pictures of you at all the places they said you were at. Probably the rest of the story is true, too."

Kenzie released an overly exasperated breath. "Fine, I go out clubbing. It's part of my job to stay in the spotlight."

Doug sang that sarcastic Brad Paisley song, *"It's just so tough, being a celebrity . . ."*

"Don't quit your day job," lobbed Maxie. "Oh, wait—you don't have one. Unless you count coming here and whining about Bad Mommy."

"Hey, at least my bad mommy didn't leave," he shot back.

Doug's emo-slingshot hit its mark: Kenzie's heart. Not that she'd ever let him know. "I'm not dignifying this." She folded her arms across her chest and made a mental memo to check Wanderman's credentials—why isn't she stopping this rant-aholic?

"When things go down the drain, I blame it on the pain, of being a celebrity . . ." Doug, warbled off-key.

Dr. Wanderman ignored Doug and turned to Kenzie. "If I didn't think this might help you, I wouldn't have read it. My hope is that you'll tell the group what you're feeling now."

Kenzie composed herself. "Frankly, I'm surprised that anyone would take this seriously. I don't even know how they can get away with printing such bald-faced falsehoods."

"A little something called . . . what is it now? Oh, yeah, the First Amendment." Well, at least Doug had stopped singing. That was something.

"The First Amendment doesn't give them the right to slander her!" Maxie growled.

"So let her sue them. You gonna?" Doug challenged. "Unless you can't because it is true, your mother did leave you."

"Did she?" asked Hannah. "Just pack up and abandon the family one day, right after your little brother was born? It says they interviewed your neighbors."

The next words came at Kenzie like bullets—rat-a-tat-tat! "Was she an alcoholic? A slut? Did she abuse you? Is she dead? Is she in jail? Did she have low self-esteem, is that why you do what you do?"

Three shooters—Doug, Hannah, Jenny, all aiming at the same target.

"Enough! Stop it!'

Jeremy. Finally. "Look, I understand why Dr. Wanderman

allowed this, that it might help Kenzie open up, but this feels like a verbal gang bang. And you know what? All you are doing is bringing out your own issues, like jealousy, paranoia, and some kind of sick satisfaction. It's showing more about you. And not helping her."

"I couldn't have expressed it better, Jeremy." Dr. Wanderman favored him with the look of a teacher giving a student his first A.

Was the interrogation done then?

Stupid Jenny wouldn't let it go. "You can tell us, Kenzie. Did she really up and leave?"

Not me. She didn't leave me. She couldn't have. She loved me.

The tears blinded her only a little. Maxie was on her heels as she dashed down the hill.

Hours later, someone knocked on the sliding door of Kenzie's villa. Maxie, she assumed, opening it without looking. "I hope you brought some killer stuff, I really need it tonight." The words were out of her mouth before she saw who her visitor was.

"Sorry, all I brought was myself."

"Jeremy." At least he had the good grace to look abashed.

"I'm surprised to see you," she said coolly, tightening the tie on her robe. "It's against the rules for boys to come to a girl's room. Spy-cams are everywhere."

"I wasn't going to come in," Jeremy said. "I just wanted to see if you were all right."

Mixed emotions fought it out. Humiliation versus pride. Anger versus sadness. And what's that other interloper in the ring? Thrill? That he cared enough to come? Kenzie didn't know how she felt about that one. She tried very hard to act as if she didn't care at all.

"Don't worry, I'm not going to off myself over the latest phony exposé. I've got a huge career ahead of me. That's just what you have to put up with." *Wow,* she conceded, *if that had sounded any more hollow, it would have echoed.*

"In the mood for a walk?" Jeremy suggested.

Air. Air would do her good. "I'll get dressed."

Kenzie took her time pulling herself together. What would look best in the moonlight? Why did she care? Besides, it wasn't as if her choices were limitless. All her good stuff was at home.

She choose 7 For All Mankind jeans, pink-sequined Kate Spade ballet flats, and a white-and-pink "Little Miss Party Starter" top from Kitson.

Jeremy didn't comment on the irony of Kenzie's T-shirt slogan. They walked in silence toward the center of campus. When they reached the middle of the quad, Jeremy leaned against a sturdy oak tree.

What's he going to do? Kenzie wondered, noticing—and not for the first time—how hot he looked. Not tall, maybe five-eight, not ripped, but there was something intriguing about his compact body and sinewy arms.

Kenzie caught herself realizing she wouldn't mind being wrapped in them.

Maybe it was the wide, blue-gray wolf eyes. Or his full lips and smooth skin. The combination gave him an innocent, vulnerable vibe. She recalled Maxie's snappy sum-up: *Jeremy has that 'Do me, I'm sensitive' vibe but don't let that fool ya. He's a rage-aholic junkie, and he's trouble.*

It wasn't worth pondering, Kenzie decided. Jeremy was taken, by a rich older woman looking for a needy boy-toy.

"I came to see you, not just to say how sorry I am about the way it happened . . . but . . ." Jeremy cleared his throat, interrupting her reverie.

"I'm over it," Kenzie lied.

"There's something real about what Doug, Hannah, and Jenny said today. I thought maybe I could explain it better."

He wants to recap the shameful group session? Kenzie realized. He wasn't about to make a move on her. Jeremy folded his arms across his chest. He clearly wasn't open to her making the first move, either.

"I appreciate it, Jeremy, but I'd really rather forget it." Kenzie lifted her chin, turned, starting to walk away from him.

"They came on way too strong," Jeremy continued, falling into stride with her, "and I feel bad that I didn't step in sooner. They think you haven't opened up because you believe you're too good for them. That you're above them. So their resentment came out at the first opportunity."

"Do you agree with them?"

"You really want to know what I think?"

Kenzie's stomach clutched. Maybe she didn't. She hadn't meant to nod.

"I think," Jeremy said, "you bought into the lie. That because you're on television, it makes you special. You are *unique* because you're on television. But not special."

The remark landed like a slap across the face. Kenzie reddened.

"If you allow them to get to know you better, as a real

person with real issues, it would go a long way toward easing their resentment. And I think it would be good for you. Probably help a lot more if you came to group straight every once in a while."

"If I *what*?" Kenzie was stuck on "straight."

"I don't think I've ever seen you completely sober," Jeremy said matter-of-factly. "Without any drugs in your system."

"Sure you have," Kenzie retorted. "That day by the lake, when you practically spat at me. I was completely straight then."

"I was in a crap mood that day," Jeremy admitted, running his fingers through his curls. "I was thinking evil thoughts."

"About me?"

He stopped in his tracks. "Not *everything* is about you, Kenzie—but . . ."

"But what?"

"I admit I watch TV. I knew who you were. And like I said, I was in a foul mood, a self-pitying place, and I didn't want company."

"Especially not my company, right?" Why was she pushing him? Kenzie could have kicked herself at that moment.

Jeremy didn't back away. "I'll pretend we're in group and just put it out there. My first impression wasn't great. I was thinking, there are people with real problems here. What's she doing here? What problems could she possibly have? She's just playing the part of a poor little rich girl."

He may have added, "I don't think that anymore," but Kenzie heard nothing but the coursing blood pounding in her ears—forcing her to have the last word. "Not all of us can be *old* rich girls like your sugar mama." With that, she spun on her feet, walked away.

Jeremy did not follow.

She would not cry. What reason did she have? He didn't say what she'd secretly hoped? She was above that. Kenzie grabbed some pages of *The Chrome Hearts Club* script and tried to read. She was surprised to find them soggy, the writing blurred.

CHAPTER FIFTEEN

> "There's no shit like family shit."
>
> —ALICE LEE

Sunday was Family Day at Serenity Lake. At the halfway point in her stay there, Kenzie was invited to participate.

Her dad was coming. The same dad, she thought ruefully, who'd brought her up, mostly as a single parent, loved her unconditionally, supported all her dreams—and then sided with everyone else when she was remanded to rehab. Kenzie hadn't communicated with him since and had no idea what to expect.

She spent the night before obsessing, scripting, then mentally rewriting the reunion. Would Dad be angry? Disappointed? Would seeing him ramp up her resentment? Would he be remorseful? Would she? Had he missed her?

Anticipation and dread intensified with every step she took toward the Serenity Room the next day. She should have taken a Xanax or Valium to deal, but hadn't. Her heart was pounding so loudly, she thought everyone could hear.

Then she saw him. Leaning against the wall outside the Serenity Room, in newly pressed trousers and the shirt and tie she'd bought him for Christmas. His hands were in his pockets.

Then he saw her.

He caught her in his brawny arms and held her so tightly,

Kenzie thought she might be crushed. Her ear pressed against his chest; his heart was beating wildly. She soaked his new shirt with her tears, inhaled the familiar scent of his aftershave. Her dad rested his chin on her head, kissed her hair. In that instant, Kenzie's fears dissolved. Her father, Alan Cross, felt like home.

"I'm so sorry." They said it together, followed by an anxious duet of "How are you?=" They smiled at each other.

"You look good, baby girl, rested."

He did not. Kenzie took in his eyes. When had they gotten droopy? And his forehead, did he always have so many worry lines? "You look tired, Daddy."

"Never could get anything past you," he said with a grin.

She squeezed his arm. "I'm fine, quit worrying about me."

The emotional reunion was short-lived, as they were soon ushered into the Serenity Room, and invited to make themselves comfortable amid the dozen or so other families gathered there.

Family Day at Serenity Lake, Kenzie soon found out, was serious, regimented, and rule-intense. Like doing group therapy confessions, only with your family, and everybody else's too. Gulp!

"Kenzie!" Maxie's voice rang out, just as Kenzie and her dad settled into catty-corner armchairs.

"Over here!" Kenzie called. "Come meet my dad."

A familiar face hovered over Maxie—Lev! Kenzie jumped up and hugged her friend, caressed his face. She'd missed him—she'd missed everyone. "Guys, this is my dad, Alan.

Dad, these are my friends Maxie and Lev Romano. They're twins."

They were an odd couple, lanky Lev, light brown–haired and blue-eyed, and tiny, dark-eyed Maxie, who'd traded her pink streaks for electric blue ones today. Kenzie's dad did a double-take, but was too polite to ask the obvious question.

"There's coffee, tea, and soft drinks." Lev pointed to a buffet near the stone fireplace.

"And really good cookies," Maxie added. The twinkle in her eye gave her away: She was high.

"Sounds irresistible. I'll bring for all of us," Alan Cross offered.

Lev went with him, and Maxie rearranged the furniture so they could all sit together. "Your first Family Day can be intense. It's not something you want to do alone."

"Or straight?" Kenzie queried.

Maxie gave her a sly smile. "Want?"

Kenzie declined. By the time any pill kicked in, the session would be over.

Kenzie had never been inside the Serenity Room, assuming it was restricted to people who were meditating or praying. Plump pillows were strewn around the octagonal room for that purpose. There were huge bay windows affording amazing views of the mountains, the sky. As Kenzie scanned the room, she noted that Doug, Jenny, and Hannah were there, along with family members.

The woman with Jeremy was older, wore too much makeup, and displayed an overabundance of cleavage. Kenzie would have asked Maxie more, but by then her dad and Lev were back with the snacks.

A family therapist, Dr. Ira Porter, was getting ready to address the gathering. Clean-shaven and baby-faced, Dr. Porter looked too young and fresh to handle family dramas, but Kenzie gave silent thanks that Traitor Wanderman wasn't there.

Dr. Porter explained the format. They were to introduce themselves by first name only, and explain why each was here. For example, "I'm Dave and I'm a sober guest," or "I'm Len and I'm a recovering substance abuser."

Then they'd go around the room, encouraging open dialog between patients and their families. "We've found this forum beneficial to families and patients. Seeing others going through the same challenges, tackling the same emotions you have, can be very helpful. Please respect everyone's privacy: Whatever you see and hear today stays here. If you repeat anything, you won't be asked back."

Which might be worth it, if The Enquirer *pays enough,* Kenzie thought sarcastically.

The Romano twins were chosen to kick off the open dialog.

"I'm Levon and I'm a sober guest," Lev introduced himself.

"I'm Maxine," Maxie chirped. "I'm like an 'everything bagel,' sprinkled with a variety of addictions."

Dr. Porter chose not to comment on Maxie's mocking words. He stuck with the program. "Would you like to say anything to your brother?"

"Thanks for showing up, brother dear." Maxie batted her eyelashes, tilted her head, and gazed at him in exaggerated adoration.

"I'm always here for you and always will be," Lev said evenly.

"As opposed to, say, our dear diva parents? Where are they these days?" she asked in a voice laced with sarcasm.

"They're performing overseas, but they sent a message," Lev responded. "They're sorry they couldn't be here, but they beg you to please return their calls. They really want to connect."

"I'm crying on the inside," Maxie deadpanned.

"What would you say to your parents if they were here?" Dr. Porter prompted.

"Fuck you," Maxie mumbled softly, lowering her head. Lev drew her to him, and she buried her face in his shirt so no one could see her fall apart.

Big Doug was squished into a folding chair near a pair of pinched-faced, silver-haired women who'd identified themselves as his mother and aunt.

"Douglas," Dr. Porter asked pleasantly, "what would you like to say to your family?"

"Um, thanks for coming," he mumbled sheepishly, hanging his head.

Kenzie tensed instinctively. This was not going to go well.

Doug's mother straightened her spine. Instead of addressing her son, she turned to Dr. Porter. "I'm going to be frank. I'd like to know how much longer this will last. It's getting expensive, and I don't see any progress."

"Douglas, would you like to respond to your mother's question?"

Doug was flushed. What he said sounded rehearsed. "I'm sorry you feel that way, Mother. But, with all due respect, you inherited millions when Dad died. And I believe I am making progress." He flicked his eyes up at Dr. Porter, who nodded encouragingly.

Mommy Dearest wasn't buying it. "Your father's estate was left to me, to disperse as I see fit—and I have significant expenses other than this . . ." She waved her hand around the room. ". . . overpriced vacation resort."

"It's not like I want to be here," Doug reminded her.

"Really?" his mother's drawn-on eyebrows arched. "Then why not leave?"

Doug's round cheeks reddened. "I haven't finished my therapy."

"Of course you haven't," she mimicked cruelly. "When you do, you'll go right back to the bottle. It's not like that hasn't happened before."

Way to be supportive, Mom, Kenzie thought disgustedly. She found herself rooting for Doug to trash his mother, but the big lug crumpled like a used tissue. "Right. I'm a loser and always will be. Sorry for being born."

"Sometimes, I am too." Doug's mother sniffed.

She could *not* have said that. Everyone in the room gasped at the coldness of this woman. Doug bolted from his chair, slamming the door on his way out.

Dr. Porter tried but failed to hide his anger behind a veneer of professionalism. "While we encourage honesty here, Mrs. Thacker, I strenuously urge you to consider therapy yourself. Studies have shown that extreme bitterness leads to early death."

Sure that Dr. Porter had just lied through his teeth, Kenzie nearly applauded.

Then it was Jeremy's turn. Kenzie snapped to attention. He seemed sincere in thanking Carly—sober guest, Carly Williams, as she'd identified herself—for everything she'd done for him.

"You're so welcome," Carly gushed. "You mean so much to me, I couldn't stand by and watch you throw your life away."

"I got lucky," Jeremy admitted. "I was really messed up and you cared enough to reach out."

"I'll always be there for you," Carly pledged, hand to bodacious chest.

Pul-eeze. *Can I get a vomit bag?* Kenzie wondered.

As more families spoke, Kenzie's fascination grew. By turns, their stories were poignant and forgiving, bitter and accusing, guilt-ridden and sorrowful, phony and raw. Hannah appeared to come from a family of whiners and hand wringers. They blamed themselves for her exercise bulimia.

Jenny's clan was the opposite, upbeat and optimistic. Her mother had suffered her own eating disorders; she knew the struggle ahead *and* knew it could be beat.

Kenzie, newest to the Family Day process, was the last to participate. Now that she'd witnessed this confession-session, she resolved to vague it up, reveal nothing. She was the only celebrity in the room, and tabloids pay big money for insider info.

Her dad didn't get that memo. He started to speak, using a tone of voice Kenzie knew well: earnest, sincere, from-the-heart. Visions of headlines scrawled across Kenzie's brain:

Exclusive! Father Accuses Star Daughter of Being a Selfish Bitch!

Daughter Dumps on Dad! "You Betrayed Me!" Kenzie Cries!

She shuddered, determined to keep it casual, saying only, "I miss you, Daddy. I'm sorry they wouldn't let me call or e-mail you."

"You probably want to know why I agreed to send you here," Alan Cross said.

In an effort to derail him, Kenzie cooed, "You don't have to explain, Daddy. I *totally* understand."

"No, sweetie, I don't think you do."

A red flag went up. Was her dad about to expose something that should not be made public?

"I've been so worried about how hard they work you." Her dad leaned toward her. "Your agents and managers, all those people. And the clubbing every night—"

"It's no big, Daddy," Kenzie broke in.

Her father acted as if he hadn't heard her. "At first, I tried to convince myself that you'd be drinking anyway, if you were away at college. But Hollywood is a different playground. You're exposed to so much debauchery and temptation! All that money they throw at you, the free clothes, and cars, and trips, and drugs—I'm not sure any nineteen-year-old could resist all that and know when to say, 'Stop. I'm in over my head!'"

"I can handle it." Kenzie shrugged, doing her best toss-off delivery.

Only her father was not about to be tossed off so easily. "When Chelsea told me you were going to rehab, I was relieved."

Kenzie's jaw dropped. He was?

"How does that make you feel, Kenzie?" Dr. Porter prodded.

"Betrayed," Kenzie blurted, folding her arms.

"I'm so sorry, honey. I was afraid you'd feel like that." Her father's face folded, Kenzie's eyes clouded.

"As recently as six months ago, it was inconceivable to me that my little girl would ever need to go into rehab. I would have tried to stop them from sending you here. But then I saw for myself what was happening to you."

"Saw for yourself?" Kenzie repeated, confused.

"The day you came to Seth's soccer game, and spent the whole time posing for photographers, that's when it hit me just how much you've changed. You've always bloomed in the spotlight, but never hogged it before. You didn't used to be selfish."

Kenzie's throat closed, her eyes filled with tears.

"That's not you. That's not the girl we know and sent off to Hollywood to make her dreams come true. Maybe you got sucked into believing you're the most important person in the world. That your brother, your family, doesn't count."

"That's not true!" Kenzie blurted, full-out sobbing. "I love Seth and you. I couldn't help it if the paparazzi followed me! I didn't ask them to."

"Nor did you ignore them or send them away," Alan Cross pointed out.

"What do you want me to do? Quit?" Kenzie grabbed a tissue and wiped her eyes.

"No, baby. You've wanted to be an actress forever. We've supported you, believed in you—your mom, Seth, and me.

We were your biggest cheerleaders when you got your big break. You deserve all the success, but not at the expense of losing yourself, your values. I guess I'm hoping that being in rehab will teach you how to live your dream life, but never forget what's important in life and be the person you really are. Can you try, sweetheart?"

Shamed, Kenzie mumbled, "I'll try, Daddy. Tell Seth I'm sorry."

Her father brightened. "Already have. He's coming next week to tell you how proud he is that his sister is facing up to big problems and dealing with them."

CHAPTER SIXTEEN

Making Choices

Kenzie couldn't sleep. The Family Day soul-baring session, witnessed by everyone—including Jeremy—played before her like a continuous loop of guilt and shame. For some reason she couldn't fathom, she hadn't taken the sleeping pill Maxie had provided. By five A.M., she was done tossing, turning, and torturing herself.

She didn't want to be alone. Breakfast wouldn't be served for another two hours, and it way too early to rouse Maxie. That narrowed her choices to one: Serenity Lake's predawn meditative walk around the lake.

Gamely, she laced up her sneakers, zipped up a hoodie, and attached herself to the small group heading to the lake. She looked for someone to chat with, but they all seemed to be taking the meditation part seriously.

Kenzie tried to focus inward, but her mind was defiantly outward bound.

She forced herself to rein it it, be hyperaware of her surroundings, appreciate nature and the crisp clean morning air. To, as they say in yoga, be present in the moment. She took in the beauty of the lake, shimmering in the first rays of sunlight, the leafy palm trees and sturdy oaks. She attuned herself to the sounds of a dozen pairs of hiking boots walking single file along the trail. She listened to the birds chirping and caw-cawing. They sounded screechy, annoying.

Being present wasn't helping.

She fell back to the recent past: yesterday again.

She'd been so sure her dad would apologize for having agreed with her friends and advisors about rehab, that he now regretted the decision, wished he'd taken a stand against it.

In her heart and soul, she'd believed that just by being there, he'd make everything better. Like always.

Instead, he'd practically accused her of being a self-absorbed narcissist. Of not caring about anyone except herself, not even her brother. So unfair! And untrue.

Kenzie felt a tap on the back and whirled around. The woman hiking behind her was wearing black sweatpants, a sweatshirt several sizes too big, and tall white Uggs boots. "You're Kenzie, aren't you?"

"I am," Kenzie agreed, squashing the instinct to tell her that her Uggs were so Cameron Diaz, 2004. The woman looked familiar, but not enough to place the face. Her hair was stringy underneath a baseball cap, her smile sad, her eyes . . . haunted.

"Sherry," they said at the same time.

"Sherry Sweeney," Kenzie clarified, sure now that Maxie had been right; she *had* been in the hallway on Kenzie's first day there, detoxing.

"How are you feeling?" Kenzie asked.

"Much better, now that I'm over the worst of it. Detox is the pits. I strongly advise you not to go there."

"Good advice," Kenzie agreed, picturing her clinging to her blanket, shivering, sweating, shaking on the cold villa floor. Kenzie had been in junior high during Sherry Sweeney's movie star years. The actress used to be robustly pretty, with lush dark hair and sparkling eyes, every boy's dream girl, every girl's role model. Fast-forward ten years. She was pale, painfully thin, worn-out, haggard. What'd happened?

Sherry saw the question on Kenzie's face. "If you want to know, I'm happy to tell you. Actresses love talking about themselves."

"As long as we look fabulous doing it," Kenzie quipped and tossed her hair back, forgetting it was under the hoodie.

Sherry's laugh was throaty, hearty. Her story—unfortunately—cliché.

It was the whole too-much, too-soon, too-few-caring-people-in-her-life saga. No Dad, no hard-partying, grubby thieving Mom. It was the trappings of celebrity, the freebies, the around-the-clock fun, the diva treatment, the pedestal she was told she belonged on. When she fell off it, no one was there to catch her. So she crashed. Big-time.

"When you're in the middle of it," Sherry said, "you're having such a blast, you don't see yourself needing more and more. Drinking and doing drugs will always catch up with you, but being addicted to being famous? That's ten times worse. Try detoxing from that. That's the thing about fame, it's a very dangerous game."

Serenity Lake was her sixth stab at rehab.

"I admire you for not giving up." Kenzie meant it. She liked this woman, appreciated her candor and her courage.

"I am not the face of your future, Kenzie, if that's what

you're scared of. You're smarter than I ever was. Clearly, you have good people around you. They got you here—before you messed up too badly." Sherry winked.

Food for thought.

Kenzie had worked up a serious appetite by breakfast, so was tucking into scrambled eggs, bacon, and toast when Maxie plopped down next to her and ordered her usual: Sugar Snaps, banana slices, and milk.

Kenzie wanted to talk about Family Day, about Maxie's family, specifically. According to Lev, it'd sounded like Maxie's parents were reaching out, in spite of having chosen career over family.

As soon as those words popped into Kenzie's head, she tried to erase them. Is that how her father thinks of her, someone choosing career over him and Seth?

Maxie's parents have commitments, way more than Kenzie did, she rationalized. Being so famous, they probably have people who depend on them to make their living. The Romanos have real promises to keep.

So was Kenzie taking their side over Max? How messed up was that?

She forged ahead anyway. Maybe Maxie needed to talk. But, no.

What Maxie wanted was to go back to Kenzie's room and get stoned. She'd scored some excellent stuff.

Only . . . Kenzie had equine therapy scheduled after breakfast. It was her first day to actually groom Brad Pitt. If she did it well, she might get to feed him, see if he'd eat out of her hand.

Kenzie shocked herself by blowing off Maxie, choosing Brad Pitt over her friend's offer of drugs.

Maxie pretended not to mind. "More for me," she said unconvincingly. Maxie was no actress. She'd been hurt during the Family Day encounter, and now Kenzie had just added to it.

She swore to make it up to Maxie.

Brad Pitt was waiting in his stall. He whinnied when Kenzie approached. Horse talk for "I'm happy to see you."

"Not as happy as you will be when I'm done," she said with a wink. "You will be the handsomest stud in the stable."

He pawed the ground.

Kenzie laughed. "Okay, you already *are* the sickest stud at Serenity. She'd snagged a bottle of Kiehl's conditioner from the gift shop, planning to use it on his mane and tail.

"This is a big day for us," she told the horse, dragging a step stool into the stall. "A real test of our relationship."

She'd watched Sue demonstrate. It was time to prove that Kenzie had come far enough in recovery therapy to be responsible for another creature. Also, to see if Brad trusted her enough to let her groom his body.

Sue was posted outside the stable, but Kenzie was confident she would not need help. She and Brad got each other, as movie stars will.

She gathered the beauty tools, set the step stool by his haunches, and got to work. "This is a currycomb," she explained. "It's like a loofah, gets all the dirt off you."

Brad stood perfectly still. Unlike the other men in her life, Kenzie thought, this one's into her. The horse responded to her touch—and her voice. "Thanks for that," she told him. That, and more.

"I saw my dad yesterday," she said, making her way around him. "I feel like he doesn't trust me anymore, like he really believes I'm a screwup."

Brad turned his head, shooting Kenzie a one-eyed sideways glance.

"Don't believe it?" she challenged him. "You weren't there." Kenzie hopped on the step stool to be tall enough to clean Brad's broad back. More dirt was packed where the saddle had sat. She had to scrub harder.

"Dad's coming back next week," she mused, "bringing Seth—I just hope he doesn't decide to talk about my mom. It'll only give the tabloids more fodder. I'll bet anything there's a spy in that room." She shuddered.

Brad flicked his tail.

Kenzie then switched to a brisk brush for Brad's underbelly and legs. She pictured the tabloids getting a shot of her doing that chore. "Can you imagine the fun they'd have with this?" she asked Brad. "Starlet horsing around on hands and knees!"

She giggled.

"Maxie will get a kick out of that." Kenzie stopped, remembering the look on her friend's face this morning. "I really hurt her feelings," she confessed to the horse. "And picked a crap time to do it, too. Yesterday was horrible for her—her parents didn't even bother showing up. And then I chose to come here instead of hanging with her and getting high."

Brad whinnied.

"Yeah, I know *you're* glad I came here! But Maxie's been a lifeline to me. I don't want to bruise her or lose her friendship. It's important."

Time for hoof cleaning. Brad stood perfectly still as Kenzie positioned her shoulder against his, leaned over, and gently stroked his leg. She then gently lifted his hoof, and got to work with the pick, removing the dirt clods and small stones.

"When I get out of here, I'll get you a pair of cashmere-lined boots—two pairs, in white, to match your mane and tail. They'll keep your hooves clean and cozy."

Brad snorted.

Kenzie had saved the best for last—styling his hair. She dipped the mane comb in the Kiehl's conditioner, jumped back on the step stool and combed through his glorious white mane until it was silky and shiny.

Flashback: When Kenzie was a kid, she used to play with My Little Pony.

Flashbulb! How amazing would Brad's mane look plaited, braided, or in dreadlocks?!

The memory stopped her in her tracks. Her mom had bought her the toy for her fifth birthday. "When you're a star, we'll get you a real one. Like Elizabeth Taylor in *National Velvet*. Maybe they'll do a remake with you in it."

National Velvet, Kenzie remembered, was a really old movie about a farm girl eager to enter her beloved horse in a big race. It was Kenzie's mom's favorite film. Abby Cross had never ridden a horse, but always wanted to. She used to say she could taste the freedom of galloping away, destination nowhere, her hair flowing in the breeze.

It hit Kenzie like a ton of bricks: Just like the woman in her recurring dream.

Kenzie refused to think about that, shook off her memories, threw herself into finishing grooming the horse. She braided his forelock, stood back, and admired her handiwork.

"You look like a hipster horse," she decided.

Brad must have been grateful. He lowered his head until the crook of his neck rested on her shoulder. Kenzie put her arms around his neck, pressed her cheek to him. "You're my only boy, you know that?" she murmured. "Cole's long gone, and I screwed up any chance I might have had with Jeremy. Not that I'm into him. It'd be nice if he just didn't hate me."

Brad sighed.

"I trashed his Carly person, his benefactor. When I saw her on Family Day . . . don't know . . . she seemed sincere. It's possible she's just a compassionate rich person who did a good thing. Maybe she's like a surrogate mother to Jeremy."

She thought for a moment. "I should probably apologize to Jeremy."

"I think you just did."

Kenzie spun around.

"How long have you been standing there?" she demanded.

"Not long," Jeremy said.

Long enough to hear what I just said.

"If you're done here, we could walk back together," he suggested. "Nice job on the horse, by the way."

They'd started off toward campus when Kenzie heard Sue call her. She looked over her shoulder. Sue cupped her hand over her mouth and shouted, "Creative!"

Kenzie beamed.

"You're proud of yourself," Jeremy noted. "That's nice."

"Look, Jeremy—what you heard me say to Brad—"

"Who?"

"My horse. I meant it. What I said the other night about Carly was immature and mean. Your relationship is none of my business."

"At first," Jeremy conceded, "I didn't even know what you were talking about. Then I realized you probably heard some rumor about Carly and assumed it was true. Which is ironic, coming from you."

Chastised, Kenzie nodded.

Jeremy didn't owe Kenzie any explanation, but as they walked, he gave her one.

He'd left home at fifteen, with the vague idea of finding his brother, who'd split a year prior. Jeremy's main destination was "anywhere but here." He didn't go into detail about his childhood, only that it was very fucked up, just like others in his southside neighborhood.

He didn't find his brother. Instead, he found people who took him in, gave him a place to crash, food, clothes. In return, he dealt drugs for them. It didn't take long to go from dealing to using.

"You have no idea how easy it is to fall into the drug

scene," Jeremy said, pinning Kenzie with a stare. "Or maybe you do."

"What?" Kenzie was taken back.

"I got into it on the street. You're into it because people hand it to you. Does it really matter if you're smoking crystal meth in a dirty alleyway, or snorting it in the VIP room of a swank nightclub? Either way, you're poisoning yourself."

Juxtaposed images of a desperate derelict smoking and a sexy starlet snorting were jarring, so Kenzie erased them.

"Getting high makes you feel good," Jeremy conceded. "Powerful, sexy, like there's nothing you can't do. *Right this minute!* Or mellow, so relaxed, so comfortably numb, nothing hurts. There's no pressure, you can just float away."

Kenzie heard *that.* More than she cared to admit.

"It actually kinda sucks that using will kill you," he added. "It won't be pretty and it *will* be sooner than later. You *will* have enough time to royally screw up your own life, steal from your friends, lie, cheat, throw away all opportunities, and hurt everyone who loves you."

"Loves you . . . like Carly?" Kenzie couldn't stop herself from asking.

Jeremy skirted her real question with a straight-up answer. "I've been here six weeks. She paid for all of it, asking nothing in return. She's come to every Family Day, been so supportive. Unlike anyone I'm biologically related to."

"I'm sorry," Kenzie said. "You *were* lucky that Carly got you in here. It's helped, right? You learned a lot."

"Nothing I didn't know before," he said. "Everyone knows. Drugs are bad. It's the first thing you learn in school.

But when they're around you—offered to you, it's tempting. Knowing it will harm you eventually, versus an instant high? Come on. The thing about drugs, and drinking too, is that it makes you feel good. If it didn't, no one would do it. But I don't have to tell *you* that."

Kenzie crossed her arms defensively, but said nothing.

They were nearly back at the villas when Jeremy threw her a curveball. "Look, Kenzie, I'm going to ask you to do two things for me. Think of it as making up for dissing Carly—who . . ."

He paused, as if trying to decide what to say. He settled on. "She's not my girlfriend, never was."

"What do you want me to do?" Kenzie asked, lowering her gaze, so he wouldn't see her eyes, which might have been twinkling.

"Come back to group. Some people feel bad about the way it ended last time. It'd be nice to give them a chance to tell you."

"What's the second thing?"

"Go one full day without using. Then, two days—"

"Already have," Kenzie told him, even though it wasn't technically true. She'd gone half a day at most without some chemical boost.

Jeremy didn't believe her, anyway. "Stay sober," he said. "With a clear head, you'll get a lot more out of Serenity Lake. I can promise you that."

They'd come to the end of the path, had reached the main campus. By a lot more, she found herself wondering, watching Jeremy's back as he headed toward his villa, did he mean . . . a chance with him? Kenzie suspected that was exactly what she wanted.

Kenzie hadn't seen Maxie waiting for her.

Her friend had seen her. Walking, talking animatedly to Jeremy.

"You know," Maxie said, "I was asking myself why would Kenzie choose slaving over a horse's ass instead of hanging out with me? Especially since getting stoned is her favorite thing to do here. Now, I see—it's her *second* favorite thing.

Kenzie's stomach sank. Maxie had sprinted past hurt all the way to abandoned.

"I had no idea Jeremy was there—" Kenzie started, but Maxie cut her off.

"Oh please, Kenzie, you've been hot for him since day one. You could have told me the truth, that's all."

The truth? Kenzie couldn't even explain it to herself. Today had not been about anyone or anything other than the horse. She actually *had* chosen Brad Pitt over Maxie.

CHAPTER SEVENTEEN

> "Freedom's just another word for
> nothin' left to lose . . ."

—Janice Joplin, "Me and Bobby McGee"

Nearly a full week went by before Maxie forgave Kenzie. It'd probably take longer before the girl would trust her again. It felt like Maxie was just waiting for Kenzie to dump her completely, trade their friendship for a love connection with Jeremy.

It wasn't about to happen.

True, they'd fallen into the habit of walking back from the stables together, but no signals had been sent, overt or covert, that Jeremy was into her. It was more like he was into lecturing her. Jeremy needled Kenzie about her continued use of Maxie-supplied substances.

"How do you two get away with it?" Jeremy had asked during one of their walks. "The staff, the doctors, counselors, they have to know—if I can see you're stoned, so can they."

Kenzie shrugged. Celebrities live by different rules—on the outside *or* inside the walls of rehab. Surely, Jeremy was savvy enough to see that. How Maxie had not been busted was the real question. Avoiding spy-cams was one thing, but as Jeremy noted, Maxie's therapists, counselors, advisors, and doctors had to know.

Kenzie wondered if her own immunity was extended to

Maxie. Was that the reason it was so important for Maxie to hang out with her, to feed her habit? Kenzie shivered, refusing to go there.

Kenzie counted herself lucky that drug discussions between them were brief. Mostly, the two walked and talked about Kenzie's newest passion, her movie, *The Chrome Hearts Club.*

She'd reread the entire screenplay several times, and found herself constantly thinking up new ideas for how to play her role. When Serenity Lake gave her e-mail and Internet privileges, she'd started a dialog with the director, Daniel Lightstorm. She'd sent him her notes on the script and her character, and just as she'd hoped, he'd written right back, praising her insights. The two, director and star, had been batting ideas back and forth daily. Some days, she spent her entire hour online exclusively with him.

It was especially satisfying, Kenzie confided to Jeremy, because she'd never been allowed to do anything like that on *Spywitness Girls*—who'da thunk she'd be lovin' the creative process so much?

Jeremy encouraged Kenzie's passion, while taking every opportunity to point out, "See how much sharper your mind is when you're not stoned?"

Kenzie didn't love being lectured. She never responded, always turned the conversation back to what turned out to be a shared interest, the actual plot of the movie. *The Chrome Hearts Club* shed light on an underground world of troubled kids, and Jeremy could relate, having grown up as a charter member.

Listening to tales of his childhood was . . . painful,

to say the least. When Jeremy's dad was around, he was sometimes drunk and abusive. Jeremy had the scars, physical and emotional, to show for it. His mom tried, in her lucid moments, to protect him, but eventually ended up medicating herself with crack cocaine.

"Family, the ones who protected you, cared for you, made sure you had enough to eat, were in the streets," Jeremy confided.

That's when the movie really came into focus for her. She could easily picture her character, Sarah, feeling exactly that way.

As Jeremy predicted, Kenzie's focus got blurred when she was stoned. Getting high with Maxie was getting in the way of working on the movie. It was feeling more and more like an obligation. Kenzie could admit that to herself, if not to Jeremy, and certainly never to Maxie, who'd take it as a personal rejection.

These days, Maxie was resentful of any time Kenzie spent with Jeremy, or did anything instead of hanging with her. That even included the predawn hikes, which had become part of Kenzie's routine, even the delicious massages and body wraps that Maxie had once encouraged her to indulge in. Now that Kenzie had taken her up on it, Lev's sister acted more and more like a scorned friend.

The week Maxie wasn't talking to her, Kenzie had begun hanging out after breakfast with the people she actually knew best at Serenity Lake, Jenny, Hannah, even Doug. They'd apologized for dumping on her that day in group, and sincerely seemed interested in getting to know her as a person. And she, them. Hannah's casts, the leg holds that physically barred her from exercising, had just come off, and she was terrified. She didn't know if she'd be able to fight the urge to run, to do cardio, race right back to her old habits. Kenzie listened mostly, as Doug and Jenny went over the support steps with her. They were going to be there to help: Kenzie would too.

Kenzie felt comfortable with them. She soon actually looked forward to their company.

Which Maxie considered traitorous.

So when she bounced into Kenzie's room one day after making up with her, with "the most amazing idea anyone's ever had!", Kenzie snapped to attention. It was awesome to see Maxie so upbeat, so excited.

"What's the brainstorm?" Kenzie asked.

"Nuh-*uh*: First, promise you're going." Maxie's grin was devilish.

Kenzie ignored the red flag in her head. "Okay, I'll play."

"We're going to an AA meeting," Maxie sang out.

Translation: That's what they'll tell the Serenity Lake staff.

"We're keepin' it real," Maxie assured her. "We'll even take their Druggy Buggy to the meeting."

"Druggy Buggy? Can I buy a vowel?"

Maxie rolled her eyes. "There's still so much you don't know. All Rehab places make arrangements for their patients to attend off-campus AA—Alcoholics Anonymous—or NA—Narcotics Anonymous—meetings. They take you by van or bus, or in our case, limo. Everyone calls them Druggy Buggies."

"Cute," Kenzie conceded.

"It just so happens that, *coincidentally,* I'm familiar with the limo company they're using tomorrow night."

"Familiar with the driver, too?"

"Intimately." Maxie winked.

"How many Serenity Lake guests are going to this particular AA meeting?"

Maxie held up two fingers.

"Got it. But what happens when your friend the limo driver doesn't get us back here in a timely manner?" Kenzie asked.

After they'd been gone several hours, Maxie explained, Lev was going to call the office and tell them Maxie's parents returned home unexpectedly, and they really wanted to see her.

"I'll say I'll do it," Maxie explained, "but only if Kenzie comes with. The office will call Wanderman, who'll say that if I'm willing to do face time with Mom and Dad, they should allow it. It'd be a real breakthrough."

Lev's next part was to tell the Serenity Lake office that, due to the distances involved, the girls would return somewhere around two A.M.

Damn, she's good, Kenzie conceded. *Genius when she puts her mind to it.* Why her mind always goes to the illegal, immoral, or spiteful, Kenzie couldn't say. Why she agreed to this scheme, knowing better, and not really even wanting to—was a no-brainer. Kenzie was being tested.

If she refused, the friendship would be kaput. Maybe even with Lev, too.

The Romano twins had always had her back—in and out of rehab. They'd been nothing but warm, welcoming, protective at a time when Kenzie desperately needed all of the above.

"One last thing, Maxie, where are we really going? I can't go to a club, we'll be busted before we get in. I can't lose the movie."

As if Maxie hadn't already thought of that.

"No worries. No paparazzi, no leaks. We're going home."

Her home: Paradisio Romano, the estate that opera bought. They drove through an elaborately designed set of steel gates, up a long, winding driveway through beautifully landscaped grounds under a canopy of olive trees. As the columned mansion came into view, walls of windows stared out at them, balconies buttressed second-floor rooms and two satellite dishes sat atop the massive Spanish-tiled roof.

"How big is this place?" Kenzie asked Maxie.

"It has its own zip code," she quipped.

Kenzie *thought* she was kidding.

Uniformed staff met them at the main doors under the leafy portico. For a microsecond Kenzie wondered if every day was like this, if coming home from the grocery store was like a red carpet arrival. That's when she noticed the motor court farther down the driveway, bulging with Bentleys, Porshes, Mercedes, Hummers, and stretch limos.

Tonight, chez Romano was party central. Maxie hadn't spelled it out, but surely, Kenzie had to know this was the plan all along. She should've been pumped! A couple of weeks ago, she'd have been over the moon, fretting about not having some cute designer outfit to wear, but other than that? Kenzie Cross would have been, "Where's the bar?

Pump up the music and bring on the hotties! Mama wants to dance!"

So *what*, she asked herself, was with this queasy, uneasy, sick feeling in her tummy? Like when you're a kid skipping school by pretending to be sick? Why the trepidation, anxiety, the instinct to do a U-ie and rush back to rehab?

Kenzie took a deep breath and allowed the chauffeur to help her out of the limo. She barely had time to exhale when someone rushed her, knocking the wind right out.

Chelsea?!

"You're here! Aaahh! I can't believe it!" Kenzie's BFF shrieked. She also jumped, hugged, and repeated, "OMG, OMG, I can't believe it!" several times, as if Kenzie had returned from the dead, not skipped out of rehab for a night. Meaning: The martini sloshing around in Chelsea's hand had not been her first of the night.

"Down, girl," Kenzie laughed, disentangling herself.

Maxie received a similar raucous greeting from Lev and Gabe, which she returned enthusiastically, crowing, "We did it! We da *man*!"

Uniformed waiters palming trays of martinis came up and toasted the success of the "mission." They'd yet to make it through the front door.

Chelsea slinked an arm around the starlet's waist and led her inside. She was talking so fast the only thing Kenzie caught was that Chelsea had obviously done some blow, too.

Kenzie steeled herself for a major mind-bender, but was still shocked by the surreal scene. The Romanos' formal ballroom-sized, cathedral-ceilinged living room had been tricked out like a cheesy L.A. nightclub. Lev proudly announced he'd used a party planner, determined to throw the wildest, most out-of-control bash on the planet. It was in their honor, Maxie's and Kenzie's.

A tattooed deejay spun dance music from inside a Plexiglas booth—which bumped up against a breathtaking grand piano.

Smoke-filled colored strobe lights obscured the ornate crystal chandeliers. A stripper pole had been planted among priceless antique furniture.

One beautiful buffet table had been transformed into a pharmacy, stockpiled with a killer supply of drugs, pills, powder, leaves, and rocks, plus paraphernalia, paper, bongs, and box-cutters to do lines.

A liquor cabinet served as a bar, crowded with bottles of you-name-it, they-had-it. Staff had been hired to serve.

"Some party, huh?" Chelsea squealed. "Wait'll you see the bedrooms—set up for multiple hookups!"

All Kenzie could think was: Maxie's and Lev's parents would be horrified. Which, no doubt, was the point. It accounted for Maxie's mood, which had zoomed from anticipatory to euphoric. Girlfriend had wasted not one second getting wasted! Already, she was multitasking—dancing, laughing, flirting, smoking, and drinking.

Kenzie was taking longer to get acclimated. The crowd just blurred into one giant hip-swaying, arm-pumping, shot-gulping organism. The music and high-pitched chatter hit her like a wall of noise. She was unnerved by the glut of well-wishers crushing her with air-kisses and kudos, as if she were a war hero instead of Rehab Girl gone AWOL.

This must be what an astronaut in a peaceful outer-space bubble feels when she comes back to the chaotic Earth. Kenzie's bubble had been Serenity Lake: This party was the reentry zone. She grabbed another martini.

"This was supposed to be a small, private gathering," Chelsea explained as Lev sidled up.

"It was," Lev answered, "until your friend Gabe accidentally-on-purpose forwarded the Evite to his entire Facebook list."

Kenzie froze. That'd better be a joke, because Gabe's pals were their own gossip line. Word would get out, she'd lose the movie.

Lev must have seen the look on her face. "Chill, Kenz, it's all good. We've got serious security. Everyone was searched for cell phones, BlackBerrys, cameras; we're all here to have a good time. You're safe. Scout's honor." His cub scout salute reminded her of Seth. Her dad's voice rang in her ears. *Seth is so proud of you.*

"Come on, let's go upstairs," Chelsea said. "I brought some cute outfits for you."

Kenzie brightened. Whether at the thought of extricating herself from the crowd or changing into a party-appropriate ensemble, she'd couldn't be sure. As she rifled through the designer duds Chelsea had thoughtfully toted over, Kenzie suddenly focused on what Chels had on.

"Isn't that the Zac Posen I wore to the opening of his new boutique?" she asked.

"I didn't think you'd mind." Chelsea sounded pretty sure of herself. "I had to have the top let out a little. I've lost weight, but I'm still not as tiny as you are."

Kenzie stepped back. In three weeks, her friend had shed, what, ten pounds?

"Fifteen," she announced triumphantly. "I'm on this new diet. It's amazing, this woman comes and brings me these shakes—that's all you drink for a week. It cleanses your body and I know you're only supposed to be on it for a week, but I figured, three weeks would be three times better!"

"Stop! Chelsea, this sounds really sketchy. What are you doing?"

"Don't I look awesome?" She twirled around the room in the emerald mini.

You look halfway to anorexia is what Kenzie almost said. Instead, she slipped into the least sleazy outfit she could find, a flouncy white halter-top mini, and a simple pair of Christian Louboutin slingbacks.

Chelsea blithely blabbered away. There was little Kenzie could do to slow down the Ms. Cokehead express.

"I got the most amazing offer!" Chelsea chirped. "I'm gonna do my own column for *In Touch*! It's for the website first, but then it's going into the magazine! Chels Tells! Isn't that the best name?"

"Chels Tells what?" Kenzie asked, even though, duh, of course she already knew.

"All the insider stuff," she replied brightly, "about the stars."

Kenzie scrunched her forehead. "You're going to write a weekly gossip column?"

"Isn't it the best opportunity? But don't worry, I'm totally pledged to being your personal assistant first. The column won't stop me from being there for you."

"No, I imagine it won't. Being with me will probably give you all the 'news' you need."

"Exactly! It's serendipity!" Chelsea, clueless, exclaimed.

It puts the pity *in serendipity,* Kenzie caught herself thinking, *needing to use me.*

"Anyway," she rolled along, "I wanted to tell you the good news first."

Meaning: There's bad?

"Milo and Alex wanted to wait until you got out of rehab to tell you, but I couldn't let you be ambushed. Even though I hate to be the bearer of bad news, it's best you hear it from me."

Has Alex or Milo quit or something? And would that really be so bad? Kenzie caught herself thinking.

"When word got out that you were in rehab, some people turned on you. No one's sent us free stuff in weeks, and . . . I'm so sorry to have to tell you this, but Ferragamo asked for their bag back."

"What bag?"

Chelsea's eyes grew enormous. "You're kidding! You forgot? The pebbled-leather satchel. The 'It' bag! The one you cut the list for."

"Oh." It suddenly seemed like a lifetime ago. She hadn't thought about it in weeks, forgotten what the coveted bag even looked like.

"There's more. You lost the Neutrogena gig. They say you're not wholesome enough. Kenzie Cola is off the table, too. And this one really ticks me off"—Chelsea zoomed from mournful to outraged—"the Juicy Couture people backed out of their offer!"

"What about the movie?" They couldn't have taken *that* away from her, could they? "I mean, Daniel's been e-mailing me, so—"

Chelsea waved dismissively. "That's on track. And *Spywitness Girls* is backing you. But the big thing is . . . without all that endorsement money . . . you won't be a millionaire."

Kenzie hadn't meant to, but she burst out laughing. Chelsea said it so mournfully, like a beloved pet had died or their house had burned to the ground.

"What's so funny?" Chelsea scowled. "Don't you want to be a star anymore?"

"Of course I do. And I will be—I just won't be wearing Juicy Couture, drinking Kenzie Cola, or soaping up with Neutrogena. In fact, when I'm done with rehab, things will be better than ever."

Before Chelsea could ask Kenzie to explain, there was a knock at the door. A couple, plastered and half naked, burst in. "Are you using this room?" the guy asked breathlessly, even as he was halfway to the bed.

Kenzie and Chelsea scooted out.

There were shots of tequila sitting on a side table by the upstairs landing. *How thoughtful,* Kenzie thought, as she threw down two. Liquid courage. She'd need it.

Chelsea gulped another and dashed down one side of the butterfly staircase into the thick of the party. Kenzie paused to survey the scene. Maybe from this vantage point it'd seem more inviting.

She checked out the crowd. Like the liquor, it was top shelf: trust-fund Tinkerbells, professionally morose models, celebrity spawn, mixed with rockers, hip-hop stars, and young actors.

Most of the girls were scantily dressed and spray-tanned. Many guys could've been models. As if on cue, Cole zoomed into her field of vision. *They invited him?* Kenzie assumed she'd feel revulsion toward the creep. Instead, she felt nothing.

Gabe was dancing with his new boyfriend—he'd e-mailed the guy's picture, but Kenzie didn't remember his name.

She scoped out Maxie. Her rehab buddy was gorging on booze and boys, like a starving person at her first meal.

"Kenzie, what are you doing up there?" Gabe had spotted her.

Better get my sea legs. If I'm gonna be here, I need to channel pre-rehab Kenzie. I remember her—the party girl for whom it was never too noisy, never too crowded, never enough.

Gamely, she went downstairs.

CHAPTER EIGHTEEN

Kenzie pasted a winning smile on her face and braved the pulsating, throbbing crush. She'd barely made it down the stairs, when Gabe greeted her with a hug, a fat sloppy kiss on the cheek, and a declaration: "You've gotta meet *everyone*, Kenz!"

He guided her into a circle of plastered A-listers, club kids, scions, and scenesters: Gabe's crowd. He proudly introduced her to his boyfriend, Shelly, who, like Gabe, was wearing a tight button-down silk shirt, skinny girls' low-rider jeans, and funky sneakers.

"Oh my god, you look fabulous!" a familiar-looking girl with very white teeth shrieked.

What'd she expect me to look like? Kenzie wondered.

"Everyone gains weight in rehab," she explained, "and on you, it'd show right away. It means you're not eating."

The remark pegged her as one of those girls from an MTV reality show, starring a gaggle of self-absorbed blondes who get tripped up by the question, "paper or plastic?"

Shelly swooped in, inserting himself between the dumb blond and Kenzie. "Gabe's made some fabulous new connections," he boasted. "His newest club is—wait for it—"

She waited.

"S-Bar!" Shelly crowed. "Can you believe it?"

"It's a real coup," Gabe confided, joining them. "Fever hot. Opening night was a party for Louboutin's new line. Everyone's quitting Les Deux for it!"

"Impressive," Kenzie said.

"It's a totally new vibe," Shelly described, "all mismatched furniture, intimate spots that cry out for conversation. Oh my god, and the bathrooms—" He swooned, unable to continue.

"Congratulations, Gabriel!" Kenzie gave him a hug. "I'm so psyched for you, and you did it on your own, totally." *Without needing a Kenzie appearance,* she thought.

"I promised the owners S-Bar would be your first post-rehab stop," Gabe shared confidentially. "They're putting together a nonalcoholic . . . wink, wink . . . Kenztravaganza."

The appropriate reaction would have been gushing, grateful, thrilled.

Kenzie couldn't summon it. She gave Gabe a peck on the cheek and a lame, "That's sweet. Let's wait until I get out, and we'll see."

"Oh! I can't believe I forgot to tell you!" he exclaimed, completely oblivious to her lack of enthusiasm. "We had 'Free Kenzie' T-shirts made up. Kitson's doing them exclusively."

Chelsea, another martini in hand and really cute guy in tow, saved her from having to pretend to be excited.

"Kenzie, this is Devin. Devin, my best friend in the world, Kenzie Cross. I'm so glad you two finally got to meet!"

Devin Leary was cherub-cheeked and bleary-eyed. When he leaned in for a kiss, his breath could've knocked an elephant backward. Kenzie ducked, pretending she'd dropped something. From that angle, she saw that what was once a beautiful, intricately designed carpet had been trashed—stained, littered with shot glasses, ashes, even powder! Kenzie was horrified: Who are these people to treat a luxurious carpet like a garbage pail? Not her friends.

When she got up, Gabe grabbed Kenzie's elbow and maneuvered her onto the dance floor. "Come on, Kenz, let's bust a move!"

Gabe only speaks 1997 when he's trashed, Kenzie remembered.

The deejay was spinning Gwen Stefani's classic, "Hollaback Girl," then Rihanna's "Umbrella." It wasn't hard for Kenzie get into the groove: music, dancing, friends, laughter—not even rehab could beat that out of her system. As familiar songs came on, she began to relax, shake off the weird feeling that somehow she didn't belong here.

Crowds of people danced over, toasted her for this out-of-control bash. Kenzie still didn't think she'd done anything props-worthy, but graciously thanked everyone, anyway.

As long as I just stay in the dance groove, she told herself, *I can do this, have a fun night out. If I keep dancing, I don't have to go near the drug den.*

Whoa! What was she thinking? She all of a sudden didn't want to get high?

"Miss me?"

"Not really," she answered.

Kenzie hadn't needed to turn around: She'd know Cole Rafferty's voice anywhere. She was just surprised it'd taken him so long to impose himself.

He stood in front of her. He looked amazing, she had to admit. To make sure everyone knew it, he was shirtless, except for a gold Saint Calvin necklace (the patron saint of underwear models, she guessed). Ripped, toned, tanned, and trashed—just the way she liked 'em. Or used to, when that meant fun times.

"I missed you, baby," he cooed. "I mean it. I e-mailed you, but you didn't write back."

"Didn't want to," she said, without missing a move.

"But you'll be sprung soon, right? And then maybe we can get back together."

Snowball, meet hell.

When she didn't respond, he guessed, "Unless you met someone at Rehab Resort? Don't tell me I have to compete with a druggie loser."

Vacuous, superficial, duh-head Cole—albeit a sex machine—really believes he's better than anyone going through rehab. Kenzie bit her tongue to stop herself from laughing at his moronic vanity. She simply danced away from him, into the nearest convo she could find, and tuned into the chatter.

She tried, really hard, to care about the new landing-strip waxing technique, the excellent new D&G boutique off Robertson, Britney's latest meltdown, Nicole's baby, who was closeted-slash-cheating-slash-hooking-up, plus an astounding proclamation (from a guy who really believed it) that Katie Holmes is indeed, a robot.

Once upon a time—less than one month ago-upon-a-time—she'd probably have found at least some of these "bulletins" engrossing.

Now, her instinct was to flee.

She would have, only Gabe pushed his way over,

shrieking, "You have to *sing*! We played this for you and Maxie. It's a duet!"

Herself materialized. Clutching a handheld mike, Maxie loudly and drunkenly drowned out Amy Winehouse, *"They tried to make me go to rehab, I said—"*

"No! No! No!" The crowd, rehearsed, pumped their arms in the air and bellowed back to her.

Kenzie tried to back away, but Gabe wouldn't let go. With Shelly's help, he positioned her next to Maxie, who gaily shoved the mike at her friend, whispering, "Second verse, same as the first!"

There was no way out, no disguising her reluctance, so Kenzie did what she could. Acting like it was a dance move, she dropped her head, covering her face with her hair, and shimmied along. The crowd was chorusing, "I won't go! Go! Go!" She didn't sing a note.

She couldn't. All she could think of, all she could picture, was Jenny, Hannah, Doug, Sherry Sweeney. Jeremy. And . . . Brad Pitt. Singing the song felt like betrayal. Pretending to revel in the irony of it was no longer funny. No fun-rony, the stupid word she herself had coined.

When the song ended, she pled a ladies' room emergency and raced down the nearest hallway in pursuit of an exit. She passed the library, where couples were hooking up by the stacks of books; Mr. Romano's office, where the desk was being used as a bed; the media center, crowded with video game players, smokers, and geeks. She might have hidden in a guest bathroom, but she bet the powder room was being used to snort exactly that.

She rounded a corner, leading to another wing of the

mansion, hoping a back or side door would appear, a portal to "anywhere but here."

She found herself in the family room. Miraculously, none of the plastered guests had discovered it yet. It was huge: vaulted ceilings, arched windows, a fireplace, two plasma TVs, another piano, comfy couches, and convo pits.

Kenzie needed basic elements: air and water. She found a wet bar stocked with Evian.

Gulping down the ice-cold thirst-quencher, she noticed something in this room absent from the grand living room/ ballroom. Family photographs covered every surface. There must have been dozens of them, all sizes and shapes, all framed and *captioned*. The largest, nearly poster-sized, was a portrait of little Lev with his arm around a pigtailed Maxie. The caption read: LEVON AND MAXINE, FIVE YEARS OLD. OUR FAMILY IS COMPLETE.

A snapshot taken on a snowcapped mountain read: ASPEN, COLORADO. WHO SAYS SEVEN IS TOO YOUNG TO SKI?

Another on a yacht: MAXIE IS A WONDERFUL SWIMMER; LEV LOVES TO RELAX IN THE SUN.

Kenzie made her way around the room. Interspersed with vacation snapshots featuring the entire family were school pictures: Maxie at a piano recital, Lev in cub scouts, splashing each other in the backyard pool, the kids on two-wheelers, in Halloween costumes, a gap-toothed Maxie proudly displaying her award-winning second-grade essay.

What struck Kenzie was what *wasn't* there. Not a single photo of the great Romanos in performance. These photos chronicled parents who were *there*: not always away performing. Parents who took their kids on extravagant vacations, but also reveled in everyday stuff; parents who seemed always to have an arm around one or were kissing the other; people who appeared to light up in the presence of their kids.

Appearances can deceive, and these are only pictures, Kenzie reminded herself. But still . . . these were not the people Maxie had described.

"Find anything you like?" Lev came up behind her and burped.

"I'm not sure what I found—what story these pictures tell." There was a real question in her voice, but Lev was not in his right mind. He started to sing, really badly, that old Rod Stewart chestnut, "Ev'ry picture tells a story, don't it?" Playfully, he grabbed Kenzie around the waist and twirled her around. "Ev'ry picture tells a story, don't it?"

"Whoa, stop," Kenzie commanded. "You're gonna hurl all over this pretty room. Or me."

"Nah." He waved her away.

"I hope you don't mind, I was just looking around . . . these pictures are—"

"Not at all," he cut her off, spreading his arms magnanimously. "Be my guest. Oh wait, you *are* my guest, my guest of honor!" He cracked himself up.

Kenzie never got to ask her question.

Lev drew her back to the party, insisting Kenzie accompany him to the "pharmacy."

"Have a little sump'in, sump'in," he coaxed her. "It's your one big night. Why waste it?"

"Thanks, sweetie. I think I'll stick with drinking. I'm going over to the bar."

Lev pouted. "I did this for you. And Maxie. I know you enjoy a little weed, some hookah, a sniff, a pop. C'mon, Kenzie. Don't be ungrateful. What's your pleasure?"

She still *could* have walked away.

By two A.M., the party had ramped up and spread out. The polished Queen Anne table in the dining room was being used as a surface for body shots. Kenzie watched Chelsea lick tequila out of Devin's belly button as people cheered, "Go Chelsea! Go, Chelsea!"

Gabe and Shelly went next, performing to the same pep squad.

Lev wanted Kenzie to participate—with him. She was woozy by that time, but not stoned enough to want to do shots off him. Her *platonic* friend.

"We have to get back," she said to Lev, pulling on his arm. "Let's find Maxie."

Lev ignored her and went in search of another girl to play with.

Kenzie headed back to the ballroom by herself. Things had gotten even more out of control.

People in various stages of undress and awareness were snorting coke off their own car keys! When did coffee tables or bar tops lose their appeal?

She found Maxie—and instantly wished she had not. Girlfriend was performing, dancing on top of the grand piano. She was using what was probably her parents' most prized possession as a club banquette. Belting out a Bon Jovi–worthy, "Oh, oh! We're livin' on a prayer!" Martini in hand, Maxie's eyes glistened lethally. She was trying to convince someone to dance with her. Maybe it was the idea of trashing a piano, but no one in the huge crowd gathered around her volunteered.

"You guys, come on!" she beckoned. The music changed to "I Will Survive," and Maxie reacted. She needed no help. She shook it, swayed, and on the *"Oh, no, not I!"* part, she raised her knee and—no, no, Kenzie prayed—stomped down with such force that her heel smashed right through the piano top. Polished wood slivers flew through the air. She'd destroyed it.

Kenzie saw two hearts breaking: Maxie's parents'.

She pushed her way through the crowd to see if Maxie had been hurt, but got the answer soon enough. "Woo-hoo! Good one!" Maxie chortled as she hurled herself off the piano and flung herself into a mosh pit–ready crowd.

It was beyond time to leave.

Clearly, Maxie wasn't having it, so Kenzie tried to get Lev to help with his out-of-control sister, but lean Lev was preoccupied with a more pliant pal.

Meanwhile, the effects of whatever Lev had pressed on her were kicking it. Her guess? Ecstasy. A soothing calm came over her, which she assumed was going to intensify. She dropped her quest to leave the party and leaned back against the wall, defeated.

As if on cue, Cole appeared.

Wearing little more than a devilish grin and boy-briefs.

The kind of body "Your Body Is a Wonderland" was written for, *Kenzie couldn't help thinking. Cole is sculpted, a god among men.* *A pair of cojoined blondes materialized just then, draping their own* *nearly nude selves over him.*

But Cole wanted what he always does: the person he can't have.

"I want to talk to you," he said, clutching at Kenzie's hand.

"Right. I'm sure talking is what's on your mind." She applauded herself: still semi-sober.

"Let's get some privacy, it's important," he pleaded.

"Oh please. You're nearly naked, you show-off. You don't want privacy, you want everyone to see you," Kenzie said.

He flexed a bicep. "I wanted you to see me. I figured this was the best way to get your attention, Kenzie 'movie star' Cross."

Mission accomplished. The X, if that's what it was, finally had its way with Kenzie. The feeling was Just. Too. Good.

"Come on, baby," Cole cajoled, and Kenzie capitulated. They took the stairs slowly, going from room to room, but all were occupied. Eventually, the only private place Cole could find was a walk-in closet.

Kenzie giggled. Cole closed the doors and wrapped his arms around her. He went for a passionate kiss, but Kenzie had worked her way into a full-out giggle fit.

"You didn't used to find my kisses funny," Cole was undeterred. His hand crept up her bare leg.

"We need to come out of the closet!" She cracked up. "Out of the closet, get it?"

Cole's hand was thigh-high now. With the other, he pulled her close. Then he did the one thing he should not have—not if he was trying to get with her. The one thing that allowed a moment's clarity in her drug-and-alcohol-fueled haze.

Cole murmured in Kenzie's ear—and nuzzled her neck. Just like Brad Pitt had done the other day.

A wave of shame washed over her. *What am I doing?* She had not listened to her body, as yoga taught. She'd ignored every internal signal and caved to Maxie and Lev. Instantly, Kenzie was very clear.

She did not want to be here.

"But it's a party!" Cole pleaded, unwilling to let go.

"There is everything you could want her," Kenzie agreed. "But you know what? It's not the music or the drugs or the size of the bar. The people make the party. And there are others I'd rather be with."

CHAPTER NINETEEN

The blaring headline greeted Kenzie the very next day: thank you and damn you, instant Internet. She felt sick, nauseous, wishing she'd never met Cole Rafferty, wishing she'd listened to Chelsea back when Chels had warned her. Had she really been that blinded by his looks? Had she been that superficial? Kenzie wasn't sure who she was more enraged at, Cole or herself. What he'd done was worse than selling her out, it was revenge. She'd rejected his advances and this is how he'd paid her back.

The story, full of teasing innuendos, trashed her as an out-of-control party girl. Like rebab was a joke to her. It came "thisclose" to revealing the truth.

Kenzie could only pray her movie director, Daniel Lightstorm, would not see it—or if someone brought it to his attention, not believe it.

Maxie printed it out:

> *She may play a good girl on TV, but as her late-night clubbing and recent rehab stay suggests, nineteen-year-old starlet Kenzie Cross is no PG-rated date. "X-rated is what I'd call her," attests*

her sometime boy-toy Cole Rafferty in an interview you'll only see on Scoop.com.

"She likes to get down to it," the underwear model swears. "I thought I'd seen everything, but Kenzie—she is scorching-hot and insatiable. That includes drinking, taking drugs, you name it. If it's illegal or immoral, she wants more."

Rafferty won't come out and say it, but insinuates that he partied with Kenzie as recently as last night—when she was supposedly in rehab. "She was drinking straight out of the bottle, and wearing a see-through white minidress. When she dirty-danced, man, every guy in the room wanted to get with her."

Rafferty says he did. "She was so out of it, she couldn't wait, we ended up in the broom closet."

When pressed for details, the whereabouts of said broom closet and just how "out of it" Kenzie was, Rafferty wouldn't comment. "It was a private party, and I don't want to get my friends in trouble." Asked if he thinks he'll continue to see her when she gets out of rehab, Rafferty confided, "I don't think so, man. That girl's a machine. I can't keep up with her."

By the time Kenzie dragged herself to group therapy that day, everyone had either seen it or heard about it

"What a sick piece of trash that guy is." Disgusted, Doug had been the first to address it. Ever since Kenzie had shown some vulnerability, some humility, Doug's resentment of her had dissolved. Kenzie's empathy for him increased.

Jenny draped a birdlike arm around her. Hannah spoke for all of them when she said, "We're so sorry, Kenzie. This is really horrible."

"It's slander! It's libel!" Maxie put in a little too emphatically.

The friends had worn similar oversize dark shades to group, who probably all assumed Kenzie's were to hide her tears. It would not occur to them the sunglasses were to cover up the bleary, red-eyed effects of an off-campus, out-of-control party last night. As far as anyone knew, neither Kenzie nor Maxie had left the premises.

Dr. Wanderman knew better. She'd approved the field trip; surely she'd been informed of the hour they returned. Even so, she might not have suspected anything if not for the online exposé. Alleged exposé.

The idea that Dr. Wanderman would want to discuss it made her nauseous. (Well, that and the hangover.) If the shrinkess decided to explore how this article made Kenzie *feel,* and group therapy was the place to do it, Kenzie vowed to personally rip out every toned, tanned, chiseled muscle of Cole's traitorous body. Because that would mean she'd have to defend herself in front of—lie to—Jeremy. While the others displayed empathy, Jeremy kept his distance. Kenzie could not read his face.

It followed that if Jeremy doubted the Kenzie-as-innocent-victim story, he might actually believe Cole's cockamamy allegations. That'd be reason to cry a river.

"Can you sue him or expose him in some way, make him pay for what he did?" Hannah asked.

"That just keeps the story in the news," Maxie told them. "She's better off ignoring it. Right, K?"

"Sure," Kenzie said, relieved Maxie had answered for her. The sooner they got off this sordid topic, the better.

"How do you feel about this, Kenzie?"

Dr. Wanderman.

Damn. Getting off the topic? Not so fast, apparently.

"I'm not asking you to defend yourself," the shrinkess explained. "We can all agree this is nothing more than an obvious bid for attention by this young man."

"Deluded young man!" Maxie put in. Again, too vehemently, but Kenzie was too relieved to care. Whatever Wanderman believed, it didn't appear she was going to question their true whereabouts last night. Not publicly, anyway.

"Group is a perfect place to vent and explore your feelings," she went on. "It would be good for your recovery to talk about it."

All eyes were trained on her.

"Does this article, or articles like this, make you angry, enraged, humiliated, vengeful, hurt?" Dr. Wanderman prompted.

"You're supposed to ignore them." That was the best Kenzie could come up with, adding the oh-so-lame, "That's what they tell you. Your advisors and stuff."

Kenzie had not been able to simply ignore last week's exposé about her mom. She'd ended up in tears over that one and everyone in this circle knew it. "It's hard to follow that advice," she tacked on.

"I know," Jenny said as if she really did. "It's sad, but people—the public, whatever—believe this stuff is true. Look how many models, even when they're just naturally skinny, get accused of anorexia."

"That's not the same thing," Maxie countered. "Most models do have eating disorders. Case in point." She meant Jenny herself. Why was Maxie bashing Jenny, Kenzie wondered?

Doug said, "If you don't deny it, people might believe you're a hard-partying slut. . . . I mean, I'm sorry, but that's what I used to think."

"You forgot to add spoiled paparazzi-magnet who's only here for the publicity," Kenzie managed to quip. There was something endearing about Doug's social clumsiness.

"Kenzie can't be responsible for what other people believe," Maxie declared.

"That depends," Jeremy said thoughtfully. "Kenzie is a wonderful, bright, creative actress. She's going to be in the spotlight. Hopefully, more for her talent than her club-hopping. It might not seem fair, but if she wants this career, maybe it is her responsibility to get her image where it belongs."

Kenzie had the urge to spring up and kiss Jeremy. Not only had he complimented her and offered thoughtful advice, he seemed to dismiss Cole's claims.

"I agree," said Hannah. "But after rehab, it won't be an issue. It's not like you're going clubbing anymore."

Kenzie took a microsecond too long to nod. Gabe already had promised she'd make an S-Bar appearance.

"How do you feel about that young man who wrote the article?" Dr. Wanderman asked.

"He's a low-life bottom-feeder," she growled.

"Understood. But how does it make *you* feel? What's your gut reaction to what he did?"

"Murderous," Kenzie conceded.

"Murderous because he used *you,* specifically?" the shrinkess prompted. "Correct me if I'm wrong, but he appears to be the kind of narcissist who could allege this about any beautiful starlet."

Ouch. Target hit. "He's a bastard!" Kenzie exploded, trying to keep the real hurt out of her voice. "He can't get me, so he uses me, makes me out to be some wasted slut. I mean—my father will read this. My little brother!"

The idea of Seth finding out—of his friends hearing about the article—broke the levee that'd been holding back her rage, her hurt, her tears. Worst, what she couldn't admit out loud was the reason Cole had targeted her specifically. That little speck of truth to the sordid tale.

Dr. Wanderman smiled gently, offered her a tissue. "Thank you, Kenzie. I know that was hard for you. It's hard for any of us to admit we've been taken advantage of."

"That's why you should get back at him," Doug said emphatically.

"Karma will take care of that," Jeremy said, his eyes kind. "It usually does."

Kenzie smiled weakly as she blew her nose.

"Would you mind if I asked you something else?" Dr. Wanderman said. "You've been hurt and I don't want to make it worse. So don't feel pressured to answer. Maybe just think about it."

Kenzie eyed her questioningly.

"The other people you socialize with, your circle. The ones who enable you—your advisors, friends. Is it possible they're using you too? They profit from you, no?"

"Not the way you're insinuating," Kenzie said, dabbing her eyes. "They help me, I help them. It's way the Hollywood works. But they don't lie about me in the media, or gossip or . . ." Kenzie trailed off. Chels Tells came to mind, the column Chelsea had agreed to write. Gabe had promised her to S-Bar. Does it count as being used if you agree to it? Kenzie had never thought so before.

True to her word, Dr. Wanderman didn't force a response. But she did get the last zinger in. "I'd like to revisit something else I hope you'll think about. Why is it so important to you to be a star?"

Clearly, Kenzie was not in the best mood leaving group that moment. She took it out on Maxie, using the only ammo at hand.

"I saw the pictures all over the family room last night. The loving *family* photos."

"Your point?" Maxie, irritated, hungover, asked.

"They tell a far different story than you do."

Maxie appeared sincerely puzzled, so Kenzie filled in the blanks.

"It doesn't look like your parents were away all the time. It seems that you and Lev are the most important parts of their life. More than their careers even."

"You saw a bunch of pictures, so what?" Maxie said, beginning to get the point. "I'm going to take a nap. You should too."

Kenzie wouldn't let go. "It doesn't look like you're a disappointment to them. It doesn't look at all like they regret adopting you. Just the opposite. You completed their family. Probably, you still do."

"Kenzie," Maxie said evenly, "are you accusing me of twisting things, lying to you? Why would I do that?"

"Maybe you're disappointed in yourself—maybe they never were."

"Fuck off." Maxie fell back to her default curse and stomped off.

Stupidly, Kenzie pushed harder. "You're angry. At yourself. I think *you're* the rage-aholic, not Jeremy."

Okaaay. That got her attention. Maxie whirled around and marched back.

"Him again." She was seething. "That's what this is about? First you fall for a liar and cheat who nearly exposed us—now you're into a druggie? You sure know how to pick 'em."

Ouch.

"You're into Jeremy, so now he's Mr. Right and suddenly everything I told you is tainted?" Maxie accused her.

"It's not about you versus Jeremy. It never was. My bad for bringing him into the conversation. But you've been acting so angry and paranoid lately. What was with that Jenny attack before? She's never done anything to you. She didn't deserve that."

"So now you're defending the sappy little ferret? How *does* the Kool-Aid taste, Kenzie? I've always wondered since I've never followed the crowd."

It wasn't easy, but Kenzie deliberately softened her tone.

"When I first got here, you were the nicest person. Not just toward me. In group, you were so compassionate, especially toward Jenny. And you're so smart! I once thought you'd make a great therapist."

"Stop psychoanalyzing me, Kenzie. You're far, far from qualified. Starlets always think they can do everything. They can't."

Then it struck Kenzie. Maxie *is* the nicest person. Except when she's high. She's still under the influence. She's gone from uninhibited partying to irritable, impatient, mean even.

Kenzie felt even surer of herself. This girl is enraged, furious. Her parents are just an easy target. *How can I help her,* Kenzie wondered, *unqualified dumb-ass celebrity that I am?*

Stubborn, too. "Max, I've been thinking. I've got one more week here. I might like to try it without . . . taking anything. It'd be cool if you'd consider it too. We could support each other."

That did it. Volcano Maxie exploded, "*Now* you're going all righteous on me? You loved the pills, the grass, the booze, whatever I shared with you. And it didn't look like you were having a terrible time last night! Who are you, anyway?"

"That's what I'm trying to figure out," Kenzie conceded.

"Go for it," she snarled. "You don't need me."

Later, when Kenzie went online, she found dozens of e-mails about Cole's "confession." A subject she'd had quite enough of for one day. Besides, as long as Jeremy didn't buy it, she was over it. Until she saw an e-mail from Daniel Lightstorm, the director whose respect she wanted and thought she had. His message didn't go off on her, but unlike her group therapy friends, it was clear he wondered whether Cole's "exposé" might have a hint of truth in it. Specifically, the part about the party last night. "Over the past few weeks," Daniel wrote, "you've shown me a side of you I only hoped was there—how smart and intuitive you are when given a chance. I really want to give you this chance. Don't let me down, Kenzie. Don't let yourself down."

She couldn't bring herself to lie to him. Nor was she fool enough to tell him the truth. She settled for the simple "I won't let you down, Daniel." She was about to write "Promise" but at the last minute she changed it to "Pinkie swear."

Kenzie wrote one last e-mail before dashing off to yoga. The message was for Lev. She marked it URGENT!

At yoga, Kenzie practiced centering herself, being present. Lotus Hall had become her quiet place, her safe place. What had her body been trying to tell her last night? Before she'd had anything to drink, before dabbling in Ecstasy, she'd felt queasy, uneasy. Was it fear that someone had snuck a camera in, that she'd be busted and lose the movie? Partly.

Simply? She hadn't felt right being there.

Had she, as Maxie accused, "drunk the Kool-Aid, bought into all the rehab preaching?" Kenzie honestly didn't think so. No one had preached, gone all Twelve Step on her butt. It'd been just the opposite. Celebrities are treated differently and the message had been clear: We're here for you if you need us, we want to guide you, help you. But the rules don't apply to you. No drug testing, even.

In this incense-filled, candlelit, peaceful place, Kenzie

tried to work through the feeling of betrayal she'd had last night. Like just by attending the party, she'd stuck her tongue out at Serenity Lake at Jeremy.

But why? She was still the same person and she loved partying! It'd always been her reward after working so hard. Besides, it's not like she'd gone to rehab for an addiction to extreme socializing. She'd gone to placate a movie director. It'd been just another game she'd had to play if she wanted to be a star.

And this much she knew was still deep-down true: She *did* want to be a star. An internationally acclaimed actress. She was starting to suspect that she might even have the chops to do it too.

But could she reach that longed-after goal without publicity? Without making appearances, making the scene? Kenzie was no Keira or Scarlett or Natalie, any of those stars whose work spoke for them. Not yet. She needed to play the game for a while longer. Until everyone knew her name.

The part of yoga that Kenzie looked forward to most was deep relaxation. Even though she often came out of that trancelike state shaken up. Farrah had made her a believer: During deep relaxation is when you feel the peace of a completely relaxed body and experience your true self. "It's always there for you," the instructor told her.

If ever there was a time Kenzie needed that—it was now. She practiced alone this time, getting into the corpse position, focusing on relaxing every muscle, on watching thoughts leave her head, concentrating on her breathing. And she did "go" somewhere else.

She went, she now understood, to where her mom is. Or

was. It was a place of so much joy, Kenzie couldn't contain it. Her mom was always beaming, proud, clapping for her little girl. Kenzie, the ballerina, or playing the role of a tree in the school play. Kenzie singing in the living room, doing cartwheels. She felt her mother's embrace, guiding her small hand as she tried to write her name. No, not write. Sign her autograph. The swirlier it came out, the more praise she got.

CHAPTER TWENTY

> "When I hit a rut, she says,
> try the other parent."

—DAR WILLIAMS, "WHAT DO YOU HEAR IN THESE
SOUNDS (THE THERAPY SONG)"

Alan Cross, Kenzie's dad, did bring Seth to Family Day the following Sunday. Kenzie's heart leaped when she saw him. She hadn't realized how much she'd missed her towheaded baby bro. She couldn't stop hugging the kid, tousling his hair, and planting kisses on the top of his head—which made ten-year-old Seth way more uncomfortable than being inside a rehab facility.

Kenzie wanted to show her dad and Seth her room in Villa Primrose. Her father, surprised at just how luxurious his daughter's digs were, wondered if Serenity Lake wasn't really just a fancy resort after all. Seth kept looking for the big-screen TV. He was sure it must fold down from a panel in the ceiling. He was shocked when Kenzie told him that TVs weren't allowed in the rooms.

"You didn't watch a single show in all this time?" he asked.

"You have to catch me up."

"I would have DVR-ed anything you wanted!" Sweet Seth couldn't comprehend that his sister just hadn't thought of it. Or that before rehab, she'd been out every night clubbing and wasn't really into any TV shows these days.

On the walk back to the Serenity Room, Seth downloaded Kenzie on his soccer team and their chances of making it to the finals (not good), his friends (cool), and school (fine), and his favorite video game (Guitar Master).

In light of their last encounter, Kenzie wasn't sure if they should sit with Maxie and Lev. But Maxie waved her over, acted like nothing bad had gone down between them, and totally fawned over Seth.

Kenzie owed her one.

She might deliver on that favor, really soon too—if Family Day went as she'd hoped. Lev gave no signal one way or the other.

Dr. Porter started the session.

Hannah's family was among the first group to talk. Her parents hadn't known beforehand that her leg casts had been removed—they reacted as if their daughter had just won an Academy Award, practically giving her a standing ovation. They seemed to get what a huge step this was: Best of all, they kept the focus on Hannah, off themselves.

What a difference from last time! Kenzie caught Hannah's eye, gave the blushing girl a huge smile, and a thumbs-up.

Jenny's folks, cheerleaders to start, showered her with praise for her weight gain, minimal though it was. "Tiny steps," her dad said encouragingly. "That's all you need, a little at a time."

Kenzie checked the time. They were well into the session already and there was no sign her plan was even in motion.

Doug's disapproving shrew of a mother, backed by his

pinched-face aunt, remained in staunch character—negative, defensive, cold. Kenzie tried to will Doug, telepathically, to ask why Mommy Dearest even bothered coming, but they both knew the reason. The righteous snob cared only about what others thought. It was better for her to seem the victim of an ungrateful loser son, than a witch who turned her back on him.

When Doug departed Serenity Lake, he'd have to look to friends for support and inside himself for strength. 'Cause going home to Mama was not an option.

Kenzie thought she caught tension between Jeremy and his benefactor, Carly. Nothing was said, but their body language was not relaxed. Jeremy crossed his arms when talking to her; Carly sat up very straight, smiled little.

Time check: They were halfway through the session. Things weren't looking good for Kenzie's plan.

Suddenly, it was her turn. Kenzie told her brother how thrilled she was to see him. She apologized for the selfish way she'd acted at his soccer game, hogging all the attention, instead of watching him play.

"What game?" Seth asked. "The one a long time ago? It's okay. We lost, anyway."

Masking tears of appreciation, Kenzie croaked, "You need a haircut."

Everyone laughed.

When Seth's turn came, Kenzie was unprepared for his simple, direct question. "I don't understand why you took drugs. In school they tell you not to."

She refused to talk down to him or blame it on a disease—which she didn't have—or fault the people around her. "I've made some big mistakes, Seth, especially since I got to Hollywood. That was probably one of the biggest."

"So you're not a real drug addict, then?" he asked hopefully.

"I'm pretty sure I'm not."

There were titters around the room, but Kenzie was clear. The last several days, she had been totally clean. Tempted to ask Maxie for some stuff, really tempted. At those times, she forced herself to do something else pleasurable—get another massage, hang with Brad Pitt, do a yoga session—the strategy seemed to be working. She wasn't suffering the sweats or detoxing. She hadn't needed substitute meds.

Still, Seth seemed wary.

"I'm lucky that I came to Serenity Lake when I did," Kenzie added. "I learned a lot about myself and met so many brave, inspiring people here who are fighting real battles. I hope my experience here keeps me from making the wrong choices."

"So you won't ever do drugs again? You promise?" Again, that hopeful, innocent expression on his face.

"I'm gonna try *real* hard."

"Promise!" Seth pushed.

"Pinkie swear." Kenzie leaned over to clasp pinkies with her brother.

Dr. Porter was just about to ask Kenzie's dad if he had anything to say, when a new couple blasted into the room, completely out of breath.

"We're so sorry to be late," the woman apologized profusely. Middle-aged, heavyset, beautiful, she explained that they'd just flown in from Vienna.

"And boy, are our arms tired!" quipped the man, a balding, bespectacled porker in a custom-made suit with a gold tie and matching handkerchief.

Kenzie's sigh of relief gave her away. Maxie turned to her. Instantly, the starlet knew her "favor" had little chance of being appreciated. Her friend glared at Kenzie.

"Mr. and Mrs. Romano, please, come in," said Dr. Porter with a genuine smile of surprise. "Sit with your family. Is there room?"

Maxie sprang up. "There is now. I'm leaving."

Her parents' faces fell. Disappointed, they still made their way over. Alan Cross hastily got up and offered his seat to Cecilia Romano. Kenzie gave hers to Angelo, the dad. Meanwhile, Lev persuaded Maxie to stay.

Maybe one day, Kenzie hoped, Maxie will see that she'd only been trying to help by asking Lev to contact his family— see if they would interrupt their performing schedule to come for Family Day.

Maybe one day, Maxie will be grateful.

Today? Not so much.

Maxie was furious, off-the-charts ballistic. Instead of interacting with her parents, she spent the time aiming poisonous darts at Kenzie.

The fact that the Romanos had busted their behinds to get there reinforced Kenzie's hunch. Maxie *was* wrong about them. They tried reaching out to her, dredged up family history, copped to whatever mistakes they'd made as parents. The international opera stars came out and confessed—in front of a room full of strangers—that in their zeal to develop her talent, they'd not taken Maxie's feelings and deep-rooted problems into account.

"It was love at first sight when we saw you," Angelo Romano said. "We'll always love you. There's nothing you've ever done, or can do, to change that."

Of course they probably hadn't seen their house yet, Kenzie mused.

What the parents got in return for baring their souls were sarcastic retorts, or worse, the cold shoulder. Lev tried to work mediator magic, cajoling Maxie to give Mom and Dad a chance, urging his parents to keep the faith.

Maxie wasn't having it. She was more invested in being angry with Kenzie than in acknowledging Mom and Dad. The only reason she didn't lash out in the session, she said later, was because Seth was there.

Maxie waited until the families were long gone before blasting into Villa Primrose and popping open a fresh can of venom.

"What the hell were you trying to do? A little stunt-casting for sweeps week? Or were you trying to show everyone what a spiteful little bitch I am, mistreating the parents of the year?"

She had a speech planned. Kenzie was not getting a rebuttal.

"It's so ironic, Kenzie. You cry crocodile tears when *you* get betrayed. Then you go behind my back and do the same thing. You're a piece of work."

She stopped to take a breath. Kenzie saw her opening.

"I told you about the family photos. That made me think. Then I spoke to Lev, and he totally confirmed my hunch. It was their choice to come. Can you at least give them credit for that?" Kenzie pleaded.

"No, I can't." Her nostrils flared. "They're just playing a part, the self-sacrificing, loving parents, swooping in at the last minute to save me. Pul-eeze."

"I'm your friend," Kenzie vowed. "I can't stand by while you self-destruct."

"You think I'm self-destructing?" Maxie appeared truly surprised.

Okay, maybe that was overkill, Kenzie conceded.

"I think you're wasting time. You hide inside a tornado of fury. Then you self-medicate to feel better, when you could be out, having the coolest life."

"No shit?" Hands on her hips, Maxie struck a caustic pose. "And when did you become Dr. Philomina?"

Her sarcasm was no match for Kenzie's righteousness. "You are an incredible, smart, funny, compassionate person, Maxie. You have so much to offer! And you deserve so much—love, friendship, laughter, all that good stuff. Why do you sabotage yourself?"

"You amaze me, Kenzie, you really do," Maxie said, shaking her head. "You used to like me just the way I was. You wanted to join the party. What changed?"

I guess I did. Kenzie was about to say that, but instead something else popped out. "When you stay so resentful, Maxie, it's like swallowing a poison pill and expecting the other person to die."

"Thanks, Yoda. Pop some pills now, I think I will."

With that quip and a snarl, Maxie was gone.

Dinnertime came and went, but Kenzie wasn't hungry. She wasn't up for mingling, nor did she want to stay in her room. Going online was an option, the only unanswered e-mails that remained were from her agent, manager, and publicist. She had no interest in reading anything they'd written.

Kenzie slipped on a pair of jeans, a top, and a hoodie, and set out for a walk. It was a cool night, chilly for late spring, so she walked quickly. Campus was quiet. Most people were in the dining room, watching TV in the common room, meditating, journaling—basically, working on recovering.

With no real destination in mind, she ended up on the path that led to the lake. She tried to convince herself that in spite of Maxie's rant, the girl had heard Kenzie and would eventually understand that by enabling a face-to-face meeting with her parents, Kenzie had done a nice thing, the right thing.

Or maybe Maxie had a point: Kenzie had no right to meddle.

The farther from campus she walked, the quieter it got, until all she heard was the sound of her wedge heels on the stone path, the gentle rustling of leaves in the night breeze. She'd just crested a rolling hill when she thought she heard a soft "hooo-hooo."

An owl? She trained her eyes on the nearby trees, but saw nothing. What'd she been expecting, Harry Potter's Hedwig, with a message? She laughed out loud.

"What's so funny?"

The voice came from below her, by the shoreline of the lake. What was Jeremy doing down there all alone? Unless, of course, he wasn't alone. Her stomach sank.

She made her way down the rise. In her fear and haste she lost her footing and slid down to the shore on her butt. Verrrry graceful.

"You always know how to make an entrance," Jeremy joked as he reached out to help her up. "Were you following me?"

"Don't flatter yourself," Kenzie parried. Then she saw his face and instantly wished for a do-over. The only real light was coming from moonbeams reflecting on the lake's surface. It was enough. Jeremy looked stricken.

"What's wrong?" she asked, alarmed.

"Nothing. Everything's good."

"If that's the best acting you can do, an Oscar is not in your future," she quipped.

Jeremy shifted his gaze out over the lake, and shrugged.

"Did something happen at Family Day today? You and Carly seemed a little, I don't know . . . distant?" she guessed.

"I made some changes," Jeremy admitted. "Something I've been thinking about for a long time, but haven't been able to do. I told Carly that when I get out, I'm not coming back to live with her."

"Why?"

"I'm twenty-four years old. If I don't take responsibility for myself now, I don't know if I ever will. Staying with her, under her roof, it's a very protected place. But it's like trading one crutch for another. I told her I'm going to get a job and pay her back for rehab. It's the least I can do."

"How'd she react?" Kenzie asked.

"She's hurt, I think—more because she didn't expect to be. She thought she was just being kind, like taking in a stray and nursing it back to health. I think her feelings for me were stronger than she realized."

"Wow. That must have been hard, painful, because I know how grateful you are to her."

He flicked his wolf eyes at her. "Thanks. But you, Maxie, and the opera singers get the grand prize for drama today."

"That was intense," she conceded.

"Maxie looked ready to strangle you. That must suck. She's been your most reliable enabler since you got here."

"Don't call her an enabler," Kenzie said, suddenly irritated. "She's a friend—or was."

"What did you do? Ambush Maxie by getting her parents here?"

Kenzie crossed her arms and lifted her chin. "It didn't turn out the way I'd hoped."

"Maybe your hopes were unrealistic," he said. "You can't hang with a person for a month, then expect to wave a magic wand and fix everything. It works on TV, not so much in real life. You can't turn into any character you want, not Supergirl, a miracle worker, nor shrink."

"So I've been told," she said grumpily.

"Okay, out with it, Cross." Jeremy sounded tired, but then he took her hand, and gestured toward the shore. "Wanna talk about it?"

She sat down next to him in the grass by the lake, and told him about seeing all the Romano family snapshots. Luckily, she caught herself just in time before blurting where, exactly, she'd seen them. It felt so natural opening up to Jeremy she had to check herself, remember there were things he could not know.

"So maybe Maxie's got it backward," Kenzie concluded. "They're not disappointed in her, she's angry and disappointed at herself, but blaming them."

Jeremy plucked a blade of grass and nodded thoughtfully. "It sounds possible."

"I don't understand why she needs to stay so furious at them. It takes a lot of energy to keep up that level of anger."

"Maybe it's easier for her. Forgiving yourself can be the hardest thing to do," Jeremy said. He sent a pebble skimming across the lake, just as he'd done that first day she'd seen him. The memory made her smile.

"So what about you?" Jeremy caught Kenzie off guard.

"Me?"

"Have you given any thought to Dr. Wanderman's question? About being used by your so-called friends?"

Kenzie squirmed uncomfortably. "What do you want me to say, Jeremy?"

"Come on, Kenzie, you're a smart girl. You know the deal, you always have. If you're gonna go in another direction—not down the tubes—you have to let them go."

"Fire them from being my friends?"

"I'm serious. I know you hate this word, but those people *are* enablers. You've said it yourself. They keep you on the work/party cycle, 24/7, your agents, your entourage—your albatross?"

Kenzie bristled. So not wanting to defend-slash-explain herself and her choices again. Not to Jeremy Haven. But there he sat, staring at her with those translucent, mesmerizing orbs, waiting for an answer. The best she could do was a retread: "I can't change anything now. This is my moment. I have a successful TV show, I'm about to make a movie. They—my agent, manager, publicist, my friends, even—got me this far. If I dump them now, just because you think they're enablers, I'll miss my chance, blow everything. Why can't you see that?"

"But why is that so important to you? Why this insane drive to be so famous so fast that you're willing to give your life to it—or worse, for it?"

"I've already said it, Jeremy." Kenzie was starting to build a head of steam. "I'm living my dream—"

"No. I don't believe it," he interrupted. "I don't buy that you've always dreamed of superstardom, of being treated like you're more important than the rest of us—that you deserve wealth, constant praise, and attention. That's not who you are. So it must be something else."

Kenzie was over this conversation. "Look, Jeremy, you don't know anything about show business. Or about me."

He was like a dog with a bone. "You told your brother you're not a drug addict and you don't abuse alcohol."

Oh, crap. Play the Seth card, why don't you? "Your point?" she said through gritted teeth.

"I believe you. You're not an addict—*yet*. If you jump back on the Gotta Be a Star Express, it's inevitable. You'll go right back to partying, to getting things for free, being treated like royalty—and believing it. The whole scene is seductive. Are you really so full of yourself that you honestly believe you're the one who'll be able to resist the temptation of free bottle service, little pick-me-ups, and mellow-me-out pills?"

"You don't know that I can't," she said defensively, her annoyance level rising to red.

"The only way to not give in to temptation is to avoid it. Don't take a job as a bartender if you're an alcoholic. Stay far away from dealers and users if you're an addict. Stay away from enablers, no matter who you are. They're toxic."

Kenzie hadn't taken a walk to hear a bunch of twelve-step platitudes. Especially not from Jeremy, with whom she pictured a relationship that didn't involve sobriety sermons. "Why are you lecturing me?" she demanded, feeling reprimanded and resentful.

"Same reason you did what you thought was right for Maxie. I care about you."

Only not the way I want you to.

"Promise you'll think about cutting off those people. About surrounding yourself with real friends who care about you more than their own pockets. Can you do that, Kenzie?"

Maybe it was the word "promise" that set her off. Or maybe, thanks to Maxie, she'd been quietly seething and about to blow, anyway.

"I'm not promising anything! And I don't want to think about it! I just want to be a star! Besides . . ." She was fighting a closing throat and watery eyes. "I'm not the introspective type. I'm *extrospective*. And you have to accept that about me if you want to—"

She couldn't finish. Kenzie kicked off her shoes and fled. She raced away from the lake, away from campus, away from Jeremy. She set out for the one person who still listened without judging her, who accepted her as she was and truly liked her. Even if he wasn't technically a person.

CHAPTER TWENTY-ONE

Finding a Haven

Brad Pitt whinnied when he sensed her. It was the sweetest sound Kenzie had heard all day, which admittedly wasn't much of a competition. He was in his stall, looking almost as if he'd expected her. "I know it's late," she whispered. "I hope I didn't wake you—were you sleeping?"

He nickered, a soft, gentle call.

She petted his muzzle, combed through his mane with her fingers. It was tangled, speckled with dirt.

Kenzie went to get a clean cloth to wipe him down, then gathered up the various brushes, combs, and conditioners, and set to work. "Won't everyone be surprised when they see you tomorrow morning with your shimmering coat?" she said, rubbing the dirt off in circular motions. She worked on his back, belly, rump, and haunches—worked up quite a sweat, herself.

By the time she got to his mane and forelock, Kenzie was tiring. Brad must have sensed it. He whinnied and rested his head on her shoulder as if to say, "Take a break." Or maybe he was saying, "Give me a treat," since he lowered his head to sniff her pockets.

"I wish I'd brought something for you, but I didn't. I didn't even know I was coming here tonight." She rested her head on his powerful neck. "Everyone's on my case, nothing's changed since I got here. It's like groupthink: If she gives up her quest for stardom, all her problems will be solved. She won't go to clubs, she'll keep away from temptation."

Brad Pitt kicked the dirt.

"Exactly," Kenzie said, her arms around his neck now. "Did it ever occur to them that my life would be *worse* if I gave it all up? I mean, forget about pulling the rug out from under everyone who's been trying to help me. What am *I* gonna do?"

Brad turned his soulful eyes on her. He wanted to hear more. "They keep pushing me, like they know I'm gonna reveal something. But I won't. I can't—it's private. They'd probably laugh, anyway. I don't think I could take that." The sobs came then.

"It's what she wanted for me," Kenzie confessed. "My mom. It was our dream, for as long as I can remember. We watched TV together, rented DVDs, we went to the movies. She taught me songs, signed me up for drama lessons, and dancing, and ice skating. She didn't believe in beauty pageants but, oh my God, we watched every awards show together—Emmys, Grammys, People's Choice. For the Oscars, we had this ritual. She'd spread a blanket out in the living room in front of the TV and make a picnic dinner. My dad was there, too. We got pizza or KFC. It was the only time I was allowed to have soda.

"And my mom would always say, every time, 'One day it's gonna be you up there, Kenzie. You're going to win an Academy Award, and everyone will be cheering. You're going to look so beautiful, just like a princess. My princess.'"

Kenzie paused, remembering. "She would show me magazines, tell me my picture was going to be on the covers—I don't think she meant *The National Enquirer*."

She smiled through her sobs.

"She wasn't some pushy showbiz mom. I was good at acting, singing, dancing. I loved it most when she and my dad clapped for me. She said we were going to Hollywood, me, my dad, and her, because I was born to be a star. She promised."

Kenzie shoved her fist in her mouth when the heaving started. "When she told me I was going to have a baby brother, I was excited. I thought we'd be a perfect family. But as soon as he was born, just the opposite happened. Everything fell apart. She left. Just packed up the car and took off. Without a good-bye, without even a kiss."

The memories crashed over her, wave after wave, one more painful than the next. Kenzie was blubbering, hiccupping. "My dad didn't even seem surprised. He was sad, but he said he should have known she couldn't stay forever. She was always a free spirit. How is a little girl supposed to understand that? How could she love me so much, and then not? What did I do?"

Kenzie's legs buckled. She fell to the ground.

"I believed in her. She was my mother."

She buried her head in her knees and wept quietly. It was only when Brad Pitt snorted that she looked up. Jeremy had slipped into the stall.

Embarrassed, she hoisted herself up, using her arm to cover her eyes and runny nose.

"Kenzie," he said tenderly, "I'm . . . I'm sorry." Arms

outstretched, he went to embrace her, but she resisted, pulled away. She didn't know how much he'd heard, but she sure didn't need his sympathy or his mocking. He couldn't understand what she was feeling.

Just then Brad Pitt, who'd been standing behind Kenzie, stretched his neck out and nudged her, as if toward Jeremy. Kenzie half turned, just enough to look into his eyes. He nickered and gently nudged her again.

"I think he's making himself pretty clear," Jeremy said, reaching to embrace her.

Tentatively, Kenzie moved into Jeremy's arms and instantly melted. He held her tightly and whispered, "I'm so sorry, Kenzie . . . I didn't know . . . it'll be all right." The racking sobs returned. She totally soaked his shirt. He held her and stroked her hair for a long time, until finally, she was out of tears.

When she raised her head to thank him, he framed her face in his hands and brought his close. With his eyes, he asked permission; with hers, she gave it to him.

The kiss was sweet and tender and packed with emotion. It told Kenzie everything she needed to know. He didn't think she was pathetic; he wasn't going to mock her.

She was grateful. Conveyed it in her kiss back.

When they parted lips, Jeremy brushed Kenzie's hair out of her face, took off his shirt, and offered it to her. "To wipe the tears away," he explained.

When her eyes were clear, she checked out his chest. He was thinner than he looked, smaller than Cole—but nicely proportioned. Kenzie caressed his neck, Jeremy moved in for another kiss. It started out gently and tenderly, then slowly got more intense.

He kissed her neck, she ran her fingers through his curls—something she'd wanted to do since they day they met. She wasn't disappointed. They were thick, but so soft. They kissed a third time, then a fourth, each time more hungrily.

Kenzie peeled her top over her head, and Jeremy caressed her shoulders and arms, kissing her collarbone.

Brad Pitt snorted.

They pulled apart instantly—and started to laugh. They'd forgotten he was there, watching. Jealous?

Kenzie took Jeremy's hand, and they darted behind the stalls. The hay stacks was the best it was going to get, considering the circumstances. The couple couldn't get there fast enough.

Kenzie wasn't exactly a virgin, but being with Jeremy felt somehow so different than anything she'd ever experienced. It was like that perfect first time you dream about. The kind that combines heat and passion and intensity, tenderness, respect, and loving. The kind where both people really connect so deeply, that it almost doesn't matter if it never happens quite that way again. It was that perfect.

Afterward, they rested in each other's arms.

"So you heard the big confessional," she said after a few minutes.

"I didn't mean to eavesdrop, but I couldn't walk away. I can see why you wouldn't want to share it with anyone. It helped me understand you."

Kenzie lowered her eyes, feeling exposed. Which was kind of ironic, given the circumstances.

Jeremy plucked a straw of hay out of her hair, nuzzled her neck. "You smell so good."

"I smell of Brad Pitt."

They broke out laughing.

"Only a movie star could give a horse that name," he chuckled.

"I don't hate her, you know, I just miss her." That came out uncensored, and unexpected.

"The star thing, then, it's for your mom?

Kenzie rolled away from away from him, burying herself in the hay. "Yes. No. Maybe. I don't know anymore. It felt so important. And I liked it! I don't know if you know that part. I *don't* feel more entitled, more deserving than anyone else, but I can't lie and say the past year wasn't an amazing time in my life."

An amazing time she was still reluctant to give up.

"I know," he said. "But I don't see how anyone can't end up taking everything for granted. Of course you get the best seat, cut the lines, get free tickets, clothes, have fans, people sucking up, telling you how great you are. Not to mention your pick of the hottest guys. Who could resist constant temptation?"

"Speaking of getting my pick of the hottest guys," Kenzie said softly, as if that were the only thing she'd heard him say, "you're pretty hot. Can I pick you?" Her heart clutched: What if he said no?

"Are you asking me to be your boyfriend?" Jeremy *sounded* interested.

"Will you, Jeremy?" Kenzie hoped that didn't come out as needy as it sounded.

"Only if I get to write scandalous gossip stories about our steamy nights!"

She went to punch him, but he grabbed her arm, pinning her.

"That wasn't funny . . ." she tried to say, but her words got lost inside his kiss.

"Yes," he said when they finally pulled apart. "Yes, I would be honored to be your boyfriend. On one condition."

"Sobriety?" she guessed.

"That wouldn't be a condition," he said softly, "that would be my hope. For both of us. No, the condition is . . . I can't be your boy-toy, your arm candy. You'll have to get used to taking a backseat . . . to me being a star. . . ."

Kenzie knew just how to get him—through his stomach! She started tickling him, the way her dad . . . dad, it was, not her mom . . . used to tickle her. Just enough to get her into a giggle fit, and always ending with a hug.

Or in this situation, a hug with benefits.

"What you said before, about temptation. You really think the only way is to quit showbiz?" she asked him later.

Jeremy paused thoughtfully, while covering her in a pile of hay, like burying her in the sand. "Not for you. You should see your face whenever you talk about the movie—you light up, dude! That's passion, that's true love, that's what you're meant to do."

Oh God. I'm falling in love with this boy.

"Is there a way," he continued, "to channel that passion into being the best actress you can be instead of the biggest star in the world? Can you assemble a team who'll fight for the best scripts, instead of getting you into the best clubs? Possible?"

Kenzie honestly didn't know the answer. She'd never thought it about it that way. She'd raced into showbiz with blinders on, unaware of another possible path. Being famous had meant everything. It'd meant fulfilling the promise her mother made to her so many years ago.

Jeremy seemed to read her mind. "This is gonna be hard to hear—but in a way, deep down, I think you already know it. If your mom wanted to find you, she would have by now. Becoming the biggest star in the world won't bring her back, Kenzie."

CHAPTER TWENTY-TWO

"You say goodbye, I say hello . . ."
—The Beatles, "Hello Goodbye"

Kenzie had only two days left of her rehab stay. A little more than a month ago, she'd considered it a jail sentence. Now? She was loathe to leave.

She wasn't so much worried about temptation or sobriety, falling back in over her head—though she knew she should have been.

It was more not wanting to leave her villa, the campus, the lake. Who knew a person could end up with so many memories in so short a time? She'd found it so easy and natural to do the activities and didn't want to stop. The same activities she'd sworn she'd never do.

She could tell herself she'd continue with everything back home, but she knew it was doubtful. Give up an hour's sleep for predawn hikes? Not very likely.

Daily yoga? She'd gotten a list of recommended studios and private coaches, but realistically, the moment she got caught up in the movie, or back to *Spywitness Girls,* she might not have the discipline to practice every day.

She'd miss Brad Pitt the most. She wished she could take him home with her, but it was his job to help the next fledgling rehabber. Plus, no way could Kenzie afford him—she wasn't going to be a millionaire so quickly.

Neighing good-bye was hard. She'd brought the horse organic carrots, his favorite treat, and of course left all the good Kiehl products, with instructions, for the next equine therapy rehabber to use. She asked Brad if he'd remember her. She took his whinny to mean "forever."

Group therapy had been the hardest, but, in some ways, the most rewarding part of rehab, she conceded as she walked up the path to attend her last session. It shocked her to realize that maybe she wasn't quite ready to say good-bye.

And how strange was that?! That first day Maxie dragged her to group to be entertained, amused. "The best show in town," she'd said. Kenzie had hid behind dark glasses and a matching 'tude. She'd regarded Hannah, Jenny, and definitely Doug as pitiable patients, fighting a world of addictions and pain she didn't know or care much about. *They* had no place in the Kenzie-verse.

They'd seen right through and past her. To them, she was just another publicity-seeking Hollywood creature, exploiting their safe place, invading the haven to which they'd come (and paid a lot of money) to heal.

She'd never expected to get to know the trio jokingly referred to as Batwing Brows, Cast Girl, and Model Wannabe as real people. Who'da thunk she'd come to understand them, and vice versa, and come away considering them friends?

It was kind of miraculous, she thought. She'd become more connected to them than to anyone on Team Kenzie. She already had a calendar out, planning reunions. She gave out her private cell phone number, in case anyone was in crisis. She took theirs.

Meeting Jeremy was discovering buried treasure. There's much left to discover, Kenzie knew that much. There's stuff about him she may be appalled, horrified to find out, but she already knew the one that trumps all. He cared about Mackenzie Elizabeth Cross: person. He'd feel the same way about her if she lived in Seattle, went to college, or worked at a coffee shop. Who else besides her family could she really say that about?

Kenzie hoped to be able to answer "Chelsea, Maxie, Lev, and Gabe" to that question, but she couldn't be sure. It was TBD: to be determined.

When someone in the group was leaving, it was Dr. Wanderman's practice to change the structure of the session. Each person would get to say something to whoever was leaving, and vice versa.

The format wasn't the only thing unusual about Kenzie's final session. The seat next to her was empty. They waited, but after a while it became clear that the girl she'd considered her best friend, Maxie, wasn't going to show up. It hurt, but wasn't surprising.

Doug began. "I'm sorry I didn't like you at first, Kenzie—and I acted like the biggest jerk when that article about your mother came out. But everything's different now, and I wish you luck—and some good lawyers to sue the pants off those paparazzi and tabloids! Also, if you ever need a bodyguard, I'll be looking for work."

Kenzie gave Doug a thumbs-up, and he beamed.

Then it was Jenny's turn. She promised not to blindly

believe everything she read. "Even if they have pictures!" The still painfully thin aspiring model thanked Kenzie profusely for her compassion and help. Right then, Kenzie vowed that when Jenny got out, she would try to hook her up with a reliable modeling agency, if such a thing existed. Maybe if Jenny realized her dream, she'd gain confidence in herself, learn to love whatever body she was meant to have.

Hannah seemed saddest at Kenzie's impending departure. The girl who could barely look her in the eye that first day didn't want to let go now. Kenzie promised a support reuinion, as soon as Hannah was healthy.

Jeremy didn't say much. He didn't have to. Kenzie knew his heart.

Dr. Wanderman's parting words were advice-laden. "What I hope you've learned here is how to stay away from temptation, how to recognize the triggers that lead to self-destructive behavior—and how to develop the skills to resist. You can find other ways of feeling good, of comforting and rewarding yourself, ways that are just as powerful, but not harmful.

"In your position," she allowed, "it's not going to be easy. Just know that Serenity Lake will assign a counselor for you, someone to call whenever you feel yourself caving to temptation."

Then it was Kenzie's turn. She'd written something the night before, in preparation. Still, she experienced her first flutter of stage fright—a new sensation, for sure. She took a deep breath and channeled the real Kenzie: the actress.

"It's just about over, my time of living rehab-ally. It seems like yesterday *and* a lifetime ago that I got here. As you all know now, I was blackmailed into it. No one gave me a choice. I was angry, resentful, and blamed everyone but myself for ending up here.

"And yet . . . a funny thing happened here in lockdown. For the first time in my life, I *saw* my life clearly. They say celebrities are self-absorbed—and that's true—but all I ever did was blindly follow the advice of everyone around me.

"Being here gave me the opportunity to figure some things out for myself. I didn't get a personality transplant. I'm the same person, just with a different viewpoint. I'll probably always be a party girl, that's not going to change. I am sociable, I'm all about having fun, being fashionable, letting loose, dancing, laughing, and flirting too."

She paused to cast Jeremy a sideways glance that said, "Not so much that last thing anymore." Then she continued, "What I've learned, what's changed, is my definition of partying. From now on, it means socializing with people I love and trust, not how many paparazzi are outside or how many free bottles I'll get served inside.

"I still want to be a star. But here's the biggest thing. . . ." She paused, 'cause it was the hardest thing too. "I want this for me, not for anyone else. I still have hope that one day my mom will be part of my life again, but not because I fulfilled her dream for me. Because I'm her daughter.

"I'm not leaving here a changed girl, just one with her big saucer eyes wide open."

Admittedly, group hugs are cheesy. No one ever said they didn't make you feel good, though.

● ● ●

No way would she leave without seeing Maxie. No matter how furious Maxie remained, Kenzie had to make it right. In so many ways, Maxie Romano had been the biggest part of her recovery therapy. Kenzie was grateful to her and always would be. She had to make sure Maxie understood that. A tiny but powerful part of her believed they could be friends again.

As it turned out, Maxie had been thinking along similar lines. Similar—but not the same. When Kenzie returned to her villa to pack, there was a note in an envelope on her pillow.

There were only two words on the note.

PEACE OFFERING?

And a pill: OxyContin, the strongest prescription pain-killer out there. Like heroin.

Kenzie's optimism was now laced with trepidation, big-time. She heard Jeremy's admonition: "You can't expect to hang with someone for a month, and fix everything."

Kenzie found Maxie outside on her patio, her glazed-over eyes a sign she'd already indulged. The look on her face suggested she'd hoped Kenzie had too.

"I'm so sorry, Maxie," Kenzie just plunged right in. "You've been the best friend I could have hoped for here. You made it possible for me to even cope. It's because of you that I ended up getting so much out this place. I know it didn't go the way you would have liked—and obviously, I went overboard at times. . . ."

Kenzie trailed off. What else could she say? How much was Maxie even hearing?

"I want you to know," Kenzie decided to just put it out there, "no matter what happens, I will always be your friend. I'm not asking you to change—that's not a condition of our friendship. I just think you're an amazing, cool, compassionate person who needs to give herself a break."

Maxie was not as stoned as Kenzie had feared. There was a long period of silence before Maxie said anything, but Kenzie believed what she said came from her heart. "I don't want this friendship to go away, either. I can't promise what tomorrow will bring—when, or if, I'll ever decide to leave here. I'm furious at you for ambushing me with my parents, and I don't know when I'll stop feeling betrayed."

"As long as you know that someday you will?" Kenzie said hopefully.

She caved. "Probably."

They both teared up.

Then Maxie took it a step further, confiding that she might think about answering one of her parents' e-mails.

"That's so great!" Kenzie cheered.

"Don't get ahead of yourself," Maxie warned. "And do not pat yourself on the back. It's not because of you or anything you did." She paused, then conceded, "Okay, well, maybe a little."

There were more tears, but Kenzie was smiling. "I'm gonna miss you the most, Maxine Romano. Please get out soon—and when you do, well, obviously you have your own place, but how cool would it be if you stayed with me? We could be roommates."

She gave Kenzie a look, like she'd just smelled a dead skunk. "In Seattle? Are you nuts?"

"No, in Hollywood, duh-head! Did you think I was quitting? No way—I want to be an actress. At least I think so."

"A sober starlet? That'd be pioneering."

"If stardom comes," Kenzie said, thoughtfully, seriously, "I'd like to try and take the good stuff and leave the bad on the nightclub floor. I have no idea what'll happen tomorrow, just the usual hopes and dreams."

Suddenly solemn, Maxie said, "You're gonna make it, Kenzie."

"Pinkie swear you'll try and make it too?"

CHAPTER TWENTY-THREE

> "At the end of the day, the only person
> looking out for you is you."
> —HAYDEN PANETTIERE

Kenzie spent her first few days of freedom at home in Seattle with her family. One day soon, she knew, she and her dad would sit down and talk about her mom, but not yet. This was reunion time, and the threesome had a blast, going to the movies, out to eat, playing cards, just watching TV.

Kenzie's most treasured moment came from watching Seth play soccer in his first championship game. She might have embarrassed him joining the other families in their silly cheerleading routine, but, hey, she was a Soccer Sister, she's entitled!

Not that any theatrics helped the team win. They lost 4–3. Kenzie treated all of them to ice-cream sundaes with all the trimmings. No question who enjoyed it most.

No question who was going to enjoy Kenzie's return to Hollywood *least*—the old team of advisors, agent Alex, manager Rudy, and publicist Milo. *They* didn't know Kenzie's plans.

She'd decided to give only one post-rehab interview; the demand for it was crazy-sick. She could have auctioned it off to the highest bidder and would have made a ton of money. Alex actually suggested that. It didn't surprise her.

Money was so not her object.

Nor was publicity. If that's what she'd wanted, she could have gone on any of the TV entertainment shows, morning or afternoon chat fests, late night talkers like Letterman, Leno, or Larry King. She could have sat down with *People*, or *USA Today*, or some other respected national media outlet. Kenzie bet she'd have been welcome on Oprah, even.

There was something to be said for being in demand.

Kenzie's goal, as long as people were interested, was neither to teach nor preach, simply to reach out to those who looked up to her, the fans. It was time for honesty.

So this, ultimately, was for them. Kenzie chose to do a real-time webcast from her site, and invited a live audience of reporters representing magazines and online columns.

It was open to anyone else who wanted to come, inclu-ding anyone on *Spywitness Girls* and *The Chrome Hearts Club,* plus friends and family. Kenzie even opened the door to the tabloids. They were going to write about her anyway, they might as well get it from the horse's mouth (shout-out to Brad Pitt).

When all the cameras and tape recorders were in place, she began.

"My name is Kenzie Cross, and I was blackmailed into going to rehab. It was the best thing that ever happened to me."

She waited a few beats for the collective sharp intakes of breath, the gasps of "Oh my God" and other expressions of shock and surprise to die down before continuing. It was an impactful opening. Kenzie had to wait for her own heart to cease hammering.

"Some of what you know, because you read it or heard

it from people who represented me, is absolutely true. I was not, and am not, addicted to alcohol or any chemical substance. I don't suffer from a mood disorder or eating disorders.

"I did not need to go to rehab to detox.

"But when we called it pre-hab, well, that wasn't exactly true, either.

"I have abused prescription painkillers, used them to get high. I drank—copious amounts, sometimes—even though I'm underage. I've taken other kinds of mood-enhancing drugs. I won't lie. I liked the way they made me feel, helped me stay focused, awake, mellow; whatever state of mind I needed to be in, a drug could put me there.

"I was well on the way to becoming dependent on them.

"I'm not proud of it, but I'm not ashamed, either. I was so lucky to have gotten the chance to learn and grow from my experiences.

"I said I was blackmailed into rehab. Let me explain. I was chosen for an awesome role in the most amazing movie you'll ever see. Instead of being grateful, let alone buckling down and getting into the script, I was busy partying. Not just busy. I was the life of the party. It never occurred to me that if I wasn't careful, the party could become the death of my career—or me.

"Then the movie director, Daniel Lightstorm, threatened to fire my ass.

"My representatives begged him not to. They concocted a scenario: If I went to rehab, and 'cleaned up,' I'd get to keep the part.

"I was furious. I felt betrayed, backstabbed, ambushed,

like I was getting sent to jail, without a single DUI or paparazzi attack on my record."

Kenzie stopped to scan the audience until she found her movie director; she needed to give him a shout-out.

"Daniel, I don't know why you agreed to this deal, but you will always have my undying gratitude on so many levels for doing it."

He tipped his baseball cap and smiled. Kenzie went back to her speech.

"I did an in-residence program at Serenity Lake. I don't know if I got out of it what you're supposed to; I didn't find a higher power, and to be brutally honest, I *should* know what all the twelve steps are, but I don't. No one forced me to learn them.

"What I did learn at Serenity Lake is so clear to me now, I can't understand why I didn't see it before. Maybe the drugs and alcohol clouded my vision—ya think?"

Kenzie got a good audience chuckle out of that one.

"I came to Hollywood, like so many dreamers, wanting to be a star. I believed in myself, and I still do.

"I was lucky. Getting *Spywitness Girls* put me on the road to stardom.

"Here's what I learned. Becoming a star is like running a marathon. You start in anonymity, and run, work, sweat, nearly kill yourself to cross the finish line. There are cheerleaders all along the way: people rooting you on, encouraging you, offering you sustenance. But instead of water or vitamins or energy drinks—those little cups *they* give you are filled with pills. Or booze. Whatever it takes to keep you going. If you don't accept them, refuse the offers, you might never make it to the finish line."

It'd not been Kenzie's intent to point fingers at her team, but their scandalized faces told her she'd hit a bull's-eye.

"I met a guy in rehab."

Jeremy was in the audience, not that Kenzie would ever point him out. She couldn't keep the huge smile off her face, though. "And this wonderful guy said, 'You have no idea how easy it is to get sucked into that world, drugs, and drinking. Then one day, you turn around and it's your world.'

"Becoming a star in Hollywood isn't just about the work you do or the fans you're lucky enough to have. It's a lifestyle, and if you're young, and like me, an outgoing party girl to start with, it's a recipe for disaster.

"I used to be the symbol of that song, 'Rehab.' I'm not the poster girl for rehab now, but I know this much is true: I came away a richer person for it. I came away with friends I'll cherish for life.

"Thank you."

Kenzie wasn't taking questions. It wasn't that kind of press conference. Instead, there was a select group of people she had to see. Talking to them was going to be a whole lot harder than speaking in front of a Web camera.

She had to tell Gabe that even though she valued his friendship, admired him, and saw him as a very cool guy, Kenzie could no longer help promote night clubs. It'd be way too tempting.

Gabe was disappointed. Kenzie hoped he'd want to stay connected for reasons other than business, but she sensed

Gabe Waxworth was going to be the first casualty of Life with Kenzie, Post-rehab.

She prayed that Lev would be different, for Maxie if for no other reason. She so wanted to stay friends with the Romano twins and hoped they'd want to hang with her outside of nightclubs and house parties. Lev said, *"Of course."* But Kenzie walked away uncertain. It made her sad.

The hardest, of course, was Chelsea. Kenzie's BFF, the "cheese" to Kenzie's "mac." The girl who'd taken this ride with her. Would she still want to, now that Kenzie would be turning down most of those fun freebies and awesome party invites? Now that she had to bring the ax down on "Chels Tells"? Kenzie wasn't going to participate. It'd be up to Chelsea if she wanted to write the column without the inside access Kenzie had provided.

Chelsea was prepared for what Kenzie had to say—just undecided about her response.

"I'm not going to lie, Kenzie," she said. "I don't want the fun to stop. But the thought of losing you as a friend, I don't know if I could live with that."

In the end, she asked for time to think about it.

Kenzie was confident she'd choose friendship over a lifestyle that in some ways, Chelsea got more into than Kenzie ever had.

Next, Kenzie needed a sit-down with Alex, Rudy, and Milo. They were still reeling from the press conference when she and Jeremy joined them for lunch. Not that anyone was eating.

Rudy seemed dazed, uncomprehending. His eyes were misty when he asked why Kenzie was sounding like an ungrateful child, when all he'd ever wanted the best for her?

Milo just looked stricken. For once, the publicist had no spin, no words.

Alex was, hands down, the most distressed of the trio. Kenzie's press conference triggered a tirade. It was the first time she'd ever seen her calm, controlled, debonair agent actually seethe.

"You weren't supposed to take rehab seriously!" he shouted at her. "We sent you there so you wouldn't lose the movie. This is how you thank us, by telling the world we're just a bunch of drug dealers?"

Kenzie, who didn't let go of Jeremy's hand, told them she was genuinely sorry they'd taken it so personally. She'd never stopped being grateful for their guidance, support, and frankly, for launching her career. But the press conference was for her fans, and others like her, who dreamed of stardom. They had a right to know the truth about her, then they could decide if they were still going to tune into her TV show, pay money to see her movie.

Before Alex, Rudy, or Milo could argue or contradict her, Kenzie got the rest out. "I hope you'll understand, but I need to make some changes. If I continue being your client, I'm afraid I'll be tempted to fall right back into the lifestyle that comes with it. That can't happen."

When they left the restaurant, Kenzie was shaking. Jeremy took her in his arms, kissed her, and gave her kudos. "That was really brave. I'm so proud of you."

"It helped that you were here," she told him. "Thanks for that."

"Are you sure you know what you're doing?" he asked, holding her hand as they walked down the street. "You can go this alone, without all those people helping you?"

"I won't be alone. I have you," Kenzie teased him. "When you leave Serenity Lake for good."

His kiss said she was right about that.

The truth is, Kenzie had a plan. She'd decided to ask Daniel Lightstorm for help finding a new agent, maybe a manager and publicist: There were many slots to fill.

The starlet was putting together a new Team Kenzie.

She nominated herself for team leader.

AUTHOR NOTE

I have not personally been to rehab, but I have spent a lot of my career writing for a famous teen celebrity magazine, and consequently, in the dizzying young Hollywood orbit.

The character I created, Kenzie Cross, while not based on any specific person, is actually luckier than most I have known. She has a parent who cares more about her than the income and the perks she earns from showbiz. Too many of the actors and singers I knew sadly didn't have that: Their self-worth was measured by how successful they were as celebrities—not how successful they were as human beings. Big difference.

I urge readers to read *Rehab*, and imagine themselves in Kenzie's world. When you see how easy it is to give in to temptation, to believe everyone telling you how great you are. Afterward, you'll have a better appreciation for those young stars (and invariably, their families) who manage to keep a real-world perspective, and have faith in themselves as people, not just as celebrities.

For more, visit me at www.RandiReisfeld.com.

ABOUT THE AUTHOR

Randi Reisfeld is the author of dozens of original series and novels for teens, including three *New York Times* bestsellers. Her trilogy, Starlet, along with her Summer Share novel *Partiers Preferred*, reflects her lifelong obsession with all things Hollywood.

Randi lives in the NYC area with her family, two cats, and one exuberant puppy. Visit www.RandiReisfeld.com.

ACKNOWLEDGMENTS

Thank you, thank you, thank you to the following people, without whom this book would have been a lot harder to write, and definitely not as good:

Scott Berchman, Erica Berchman, Dana Berchman, and Andi Mason, my go-to crew for keeping me current and accurate on the entertainment scene. Thank you, guys, most of all, for your enthusiasm, and taking that extra step of really explaining—it's so appreciated!

Kristin Earhart for everything equine, and also for taking the time to really explain, as opposed to sending me on an Internet research trip.

HB Gilmour, Susie Singer Gordon, Tom Mason & Dan Danko & the Hollywood crew: you know how you helped, and trust me, it was all appreciated, and crucial.

The Integral Yoga Institute of Fair Lawn, New Jersey, and my wonderful instructor, Premajyouthi Devi; thank you for opening new vistas to me.

My fabulous author group—whose books I urge all readers to pick up—Robin Wasserman, Helen Perelman, Laura Dower, Todd Strasser, and Peter Lerangis, for being there creatively when I needed it most.